NIRIBU SCROLL

ELAINE McNALLY

Copyright © 2022 Elaine McNally.

All rights reserved. No part of this book may be reproduced, stored, or transmitted by any means—whether auditory, graphic, mechanical, or electronic—without written permission of both publisher and author, except in the case of brief excerpts used in critical articles and reviews. Unauthorized reproduction of any part of this work is illegal and is punishable by law.

ISBN: 979-8-88640-247-6 (sc)
ISBN: 979-8-88640-248-3 (hc)
ISBN: 979-8-88640-249-0 (e)

Because of the dynamic nature of the Internet, any web addresses or links contained in this book may have changed since publication and may no longer be valid. The views expressed in this work are solely those of the author and do not necessarily reflect the views of the publisher, and the publisher hereby disclaims any responsibility for them.

One Galleria Blvd., Suite 1900, Metairie, LA 70001
1-888-421-2397

Chapter 1

Running frantically through the alley in the warehouse district until he came to a dead-end wall, only then did Travis turn to look back. He saw no one but could hear the pounding of sprinting feet. He gazed at the wall before him. Too high! He quickly scanned the area for a hiding place. In the shadows of the alley, he nervously checked behind him for his pursuers. Panic gripped him like a cellophane wrap wound tightly over his face. His breathing was shallow and rapid.

With fingers clutching for handholds in the wall, he reached up for the most meager grip and pulled himself up the brick wall. Losing his footing, he slid back down. He tried again, this time with more effort in clawing into the wall. This time he slid back down, scraping his knee. Sweat formed on his brow, and his palms were wet. Wiping his hands off onto his pants, heart racing, he was about to try again. Adrenaline, fueled by fear, surged. Either he was going to scale the wall before they got to him, or he would have to turn and face them.

Now noticing a door on the right in the gloom, he quickly tried the handle. No luck! Pulling a credit card out of his pocket, he slid it down through the crack, over the bolt, and the door opened. Astonished at his good fortune, Travis gleefully slipped into the room, closing and re-locking the door behind him.

In the pitch-black darkness, he felt his way around. Groping with his hands out before him, he felt nothing but air. Still not feeling safe, he laid his back against the door and listened hard, fearful his panting would be heard. His heart was hammering so loud he could hardly hear himself think, let alone make out any sounds. Hearing them come closer, he held his breath. As his eyes adjusted to the darkness, he glanced around, and he could make out a heavy beam board used to bolt the door from forced entry. He quietly slid it into place and put his ear to the door.

The doorknob rattled. It jiggled before Travis's nose, jarring him, and with eyes wide, he froze. The muffled sounds of conversation leaked through the door, but he could not make out what they were saying over the clamor of his heart. Using the credit card, the lock clicked unlocked with an echo that resonated through the quiet room. A challenging shove against the door was stopped by the beam, and it didn't budge, and a muffled grunt on the other side was all Travis could make out.

A second more decisive shove against the door and curses followed the attempt to gain entrance. The silence that followed held its own breath as eternity waited for a response.

Travis was worried. Were they listening for him? He could not hear any sounds. Had they left? After a little while, which seemed to him to take forever, he finally listened to the sound of feet moving away and growing distant.

It went eerily silent. Finally, Travis let out the breath he had been holding as his body slumped. He wasn't sure if they had left for good, though. But for the moment, he felt safe enough to breathe a little easier.

His eyes adjusted better now, and he could see further into the room and make out a warehouse converted into an extensive spacious suite. Whoever lived here had accumulated a tremendous amount of books, many old books from what he could see. It was like a vast library. Piles of files overflowed from a grand old oak desk in front of the bookshelves to a planked floor. In another corner was a computer on a credenza with nary a piece of paper near it. Surveying his surroundings, he spotted the phone over by an old overstuffed sofa in front of a fireplace. Now he was getting somewhere, he thought as he ran over to it.

He tried to call on the phone but found it disconnected. It was just his luck. His cell phone had fallen on the street and shattered irreparably into a million pieces while he was on the run. He tried the computer, but it was down. Climbing up on a ladder he found in a corner, he peeked out the high-placed window and could barely see into the alleyway. One thug was snooping behind the garbage bin, checking behind a discarded crate. Then the man moved further down to rattling another door on the other side and one more window before turning to look back down the alley in one last sweeping check of the area before moving on.

Travis was batting a thousand at the moment, but there seemed to be no way out any time soon. The windows allowed a little moonlight and some street lighting into the room. It wasn't much, but as his eyes adjusted, he saw more and more of the room that was now his safe haven. Worked his way around the room. He checked for other exits from the building, maybe a window that he could use or anything else that even remotely would help him out of his current predicament. The only other door he had found had been welded shut. So he returned to the library area.

He lifted a book lying on the lamp stand beside an overstuffed chair and glanced at the notes on the desk, looking for clues as to who might live here. He tried to get a sense of who was the owner, and whoever lived here was a researcher of sorts. He charted the whereabouts of some ancient scrolls from the Alexandria library. Behind a stack of books, he noticed the man's Doctorate in Archaeology framed and covered with cobwebs. At least now he knew the man's name, James E. Holden.

So where was Professor James Holden, and when will he return? Going over to the kitchenette, Travis saw sticky notes on the refrigerator door. Glancing over them, he found the name and phone number of a local pizzeria that delivers and a message with the title Doggies Heavenly Hotel with a reminder to drop Sheldon off before four with a date of yesterday.

His stomach growled with loud, obnoxious sounds, reminding Travis he had not eaten since this morning. He ignored it. He noticed a notepad on a string beside the old dial telephone hanging on the wall in the kitchen. The note pad caught light reflecting in from one of the windows. After giving it a closer look, Travis guessed he could make out some very definitive etch marks on it. Travis took a pencil and shaded the paper until the lettering showed up. He could make out flight information. From what was written on the notepad, it looked like Professor Holden had taken off on a flight to Cairo, Egypt, via Paris, France. Based on the plane schedule, he would not be due back for another two weeks.

Travis returned to the window to see if he could spot his pursuers. Sure enough, one of them just walked past the opening to the alley and stopped to slightly lean forward to look left and subsequently right with a deep silent stare as if concentrating on catching movement in the passage before moving on. It dawned on him. This was the gang's regular turf, and those who had been chasing him were not going to give up any time soon.

They would be watching for him to emerge from his hiding place. He decided it just might be safer if he hung around this place, at least, stay put until the heat died down or a way of escape came to him.

Travis knew they were earnest about finding him and figured he would be here awhile. His stomach gave a protesting grumble loud enough to echo through the room. He tiptoed back to the kitchen and, upon opening up the refrigerator. There he found the necessary ingredients for a first-rate sandwich.

Making a small notation on the notepad, he took out five dollars to pay for the fixings and paperclipped it to the note. Then he made a sandwich and found himself a drink.

He looked down at his culinary creation and, as he lifted up his shirt and pointed to his six-pack, said to the plate of food, "Get in my belly!"

It was a ritual he picked from when he was very young. His mother would poke his little belly as she held up the spoonful, encouraging him to eat. One of the few memories he had of his mother.

Mildly chuckling to himself, he gathered up the fixings and headed to the old overstuffed sofa. Making himself comfortable on the couch, he looked around at his new accommodations. There was no TV, one radio, the library, its desk, and very little else. This old warehouse was perfect for an absent-minded professor living in a library with the bare essentials for study, food, and rest.

Grabbing some handy notes on the coffee table and quickly reading, he spotted a notation on what sounded like a description of a severe solar flare. Now his interest was piqued. Amazement crossed his face as it occurred to him, only the night before he had spent at his class professor's place discussing such an occurrence.

Travis recognized that the research he was reading was an archaeology study of the Middle East way back. Travis categorized it in his mind as a curious coincidence that included a perfect description of a solar flare. Too nervous to actually get more comfortable, every sound made him jumpy. He moved back to the kitchen, which was further in the warehouse, and found more light from the glow of street light casting its shine against the cupboard where he could read the papers. He leaned up against the kitchen counter and took another huge bite into his sandwich, and tried to make out the professor's handwritten note when he spotted a couple of sticky notes had fallen to the floor.

Picking them up, he saw Niribu circled with a question mark on it. There was another notation on the side; it had Alexandria Library unlined with 546 AD? From what Travis could remember about the Alexandria library was that it was famous for its legendary accumulation of the world's most extensive collection of books of its time.

Putting the notes back up on the refrigerator and moving over to the coffee table while finishing up his sandwich and drink, Travis continued to glance over the various papers. One ancient documentation was on a thief making off with some of the scrolls during the fire, but no trace of the stolen articles or if the thief had ever been found.

Travis heard a trash can clattering to the ground, some hollering, and the sounds of a scuffle through the window. He dropped the papers to go check on what was happening in the alley. Some bum was getting roughed up and shoved out onto the street by his three pursuers. The tramp was booted and mocked as he shuffled along, pushing his grocery cart full of his cherished possessions. Travis had seen enough and quietly returned to surveying his new surroundings.

Another document Travis picked up gave the thief a name. Hezron, the librarian, had run out of the burning building with the scroll. At the bottom of the page was scribbled notation X452P, a soldier reported to King Alexandria about sighting Hezron headed north. The following page was a photocopy of the fragmented document X452P. It seems to be a scribe writing about the meeting between the King and the soldier who was unable to catch up with Hezron in confusion and lost sight of him after he had darted around a corner and into the crowded street.

Travis put the papers down and wandered around the room to the window to peek out again. Much to his agitation, one man had stationed himself at the far entrance end of the alley. Like a restless tiger in a cage, Travis paced. After sitting briefly, he randomly checked out the library of books, grabbing the odd book here and there, flipping through the pages, but nothing more caught his eye.

A weather broadcast interrupted the music and caught his attention. "We should be experiencing unusual weather over the next few weeks with sightings of auras in the sky, storms coming in fast, maybe even some earthquakes in different parts of the country. So please stock up on emergency supplies." And on went the report with contact information, suggesting where to go in case of an emergency and indicating what supplies would be needed, at which point Travis lost interest.

He went over to the ladder, climbed up, and peeked out to see if he could spot anyone. Crap, a guy was leaning against the wall at the entrance to the alley, smoking a cigarette. With the litter of cigarette butts at the guy's feet, Travis knew this man was stationed there to watch.

Just as the guy turned to look up towards the window, Travis snapped back out of sight, tipping over the ladder he was standing on.

"Oh, crap," he swore under his breath, grabbing with flailing hands the window shade cord and quickly letting go before he took the shades down with him. He somehow managed to land on his feet and was even able to catch the ladder before it landed on the concrete flooring.

"Wheee!" he breathed, with one hand on his quickly beating heart. After setting the ladder back up on its feet, his other hand moved onto his forehead. That was too close. In fact, that was so close, wiping the perspiration from his hands and forehead onto his pants. Once he got his breath and thoughts back together, he listened quietly until he was again confident he had not exposed himself or his hiding place. Only afterward did he breathe easy.

Peering between the slats of the Venetian blind out into the street, he could see one of the hoodlums standing on the street corner. Travis let the blind close. So now he was sitting in someone else's lounging robe, eating his food and reading his studies.

Obviously, this man was into historical documents, specifically about the Middle East. One such story came from a copy of a manuscript translated from a scroll he was currently holding in his hands. In reading one set of notes, it stated that when Hezron visited Spain with his accounts of his tribe being one of the lost tribes, it caused a great stir, based on several sources, among the Jews of that region.

As Travis quickly scanned the other papers and speedreading sections, he concluded that this man was an incredible storyteller. Travis put down the article and got up to see if he could see the thugs. Travis was so caught up in reading he had almost forgotten why he was even here in the first place. Peeking out the window, one of the guys came into view, and another joined him from the opposite direction. All he could see was gesturing and pointing, but definitely giving him the impression that they had increased the search area. Just his luck; this seemed to be the area that they liked to loiter around.

Dawn was now starting to brighten the windows, and he could hear the morning activities outside. Not much at first as the garbage men move into the alley with their big truck beeping as it backed up to pick up the big bin with its clamoring and thuds of the lid against itself as the truck hydraulics' grunt and grind under strain. Travis jumped up on the ladder to again get another look at his situation.

Below, there stood the murderer looking directly up at him. Shocked at being spotted, he flattened himself against the wall. He could hear the garbage truck move on out of the alley, the door getting a serious rattle, shake, kick and thud, before he listened to the scrambling sounds up on the trash bin. Glass above his head was shattered, spraying him with shards and he could see an arm with a gun poking through up to the gunman's elbow. Panic gripped him.

He heard the whoop of a police siren and someone calling out, "NYPD, freeze, mister." The gun was swiftly withdrawn, and an exchange of gunfire echoed through the alley. Sounds of a scuffle, grunts, rattling and banging, and a police officer reporting on his radio "B&E in progress" and continued muffled verbiage barely heard, which Travis could only interpret as the officer calling in, giving the address and asking for backup. Travis waited.

It didn't take long. Pounding on the door abruptly galvanized Travis, "NYPD" was the sweetest sound he had heard all night. He suddenly felt drained, and his shoulders sagged in relief. "Coming," Travis called out as he made his way over to the door to open it.

Chapter 2

Catching the flight from New York to Paris, Professor James Holden settled into his seat and got his notes to review. He was going to use this stop over to check out some new information he had just received by fax. With glasses on his nose and the papers before him, reading and made notes as thoughts crossed his mind. He believed the latest information he received by fax warranted this trip. He knew it was going to be a long flight. He was fortunate enough to have an empty seat next to him, so he could bring the necessary books and notes out of the satchel and lay them down next to him. Going through the letters, he frowned and started to dig further, but some papers seemed missing. They were vital to the current trip and, if his memory served him right, on something Professor Goldberg had said at the last seminar.

Professor Goldberg was an old friend of Professor Holden since their college days. While their interests were in the Middle East, they both concentrated on different study aspects. Now James was beginning to believe there was a connection between what Professor Goldberg found and his current research project. Professor Goldberg indicated his latest findings at the recent archeology site dig at his seminar. He had turned up something that Professor James Holden felt may be related to his research. Going through his notes more slowly and read every sticky note making sure not to miss a thing, yet despite everything, it could not be found. After some more panic rummaging through his satchel, he realized he must have left it behind. Grabbing the airline phone, he called his son, John. It rang for what seemed to be forever before someone answered at the other end.

"Hi John, it is your father here. Could I ask you to do me a favor? I am heading to Egypt, and after that, I will be traveling through the country and landing eventually in Jerusalem. I was wondering if you could go to my place, and on my desk, you will find three files on the left upper corner labeled, 'Hezron, Egypt, and Professor Goldberg Seminar' and give me a call. There are some things I want you to look up for me," James said without preamble.

Groggily John said, "Dad, do you know what time it is? What are you doing taking a red-eye flight anywhere?" he muttered into the phone, opening one eye to see the time on his alarm clock. Rolling his eyes as if to say, 'You have got to be kidding me,' before throwing an arm over his eyes and refusing to give the phone his full attention.

"I decided this was just as good a time as any to get going. Could you pick up those files? I forgot. Please, for me, this morning, when you get up?" James persisted.

"Sure, Dad, first thing this morning, when I wake up, I will go down and find those notes for you. I wished you had waited until my spring break so we could go together. Now can I go back to sleep?" Grumpy from having to continue to talk at this odd hour and irritated that his father couldn't have waited for him, John wanted to hang up the phone.

"Thanks, and sorry, but my mind was on other things. I am not used to having others with me on these research trips. Hey, again, sorry for disturbing you. Go back to sleep, and we will talk later, OK?" James said with apologies in his voice. But all James heard was a click in his ear, which caused him to look at the phone and listen again before placing it back on its cradle.

John had grown up not knowing his father until recently when his father ran into his mother and found out about his existence. Father was caught up in another research trip, which swept them both up rather quickly and cemented good father-son relations ever since. John had now switched majors and universities so he could take some classes and be of assistance to his father's current research. He took a side course at another university so he could have access to the culture and religious aspects of Judaism. John actually was looking forward to following in his father's footsteps. He greatly admired his father for all his accomplishments and was looking forward to joining him during spring break on this research trip. John's latest research was about the Order of Melchizedek mentioned in some of the documents his father had on Hezron.

The young man was too tired after a grueling week of mid-terms to deal with midnight phone calls. He barely remembered receiving the call or even hanging up as he dropped back off to sleep.

James was a man from 'before the age of computers, and while he did use the computer at the University on occasion, handwritten notes were his mode. But he abundantly made use of the sticky notes, which could be seen everywhere on his files, books, and papers. In fact, he hired young apprentices to do the computer entries when, for example, the University required printed documents or research data to be available on the University network. It was the campus joke. He knew they laughed at his confusing array of sticky notes. They had to not only decipher but place them in proper context. They also presented them in dissertations and other scholarly works for the Professor. Comic relief was the only way the students could survive the ordeal. It was worth the extra credit even though the Professor forever corrected their work with more sticky notes.

The flight attendant brought the drinks down the aisle, shortly followed by another flight attendant who served the food. James set aside his papers to clear a space on the pull-down table for the food and drink. Followed by a nodding "Thank you" to the flight attendants, each in their turn as they served him, he settled in with the material he did have with him.

As far as he could calculate, it looked like there may be more clues at the Istanbul Monastery library. There was a notation in his notes to check out a rare book, one said to be a translation from King Alexander's high priest sacred scrolls. He was unsure how it all played in, but he had suspicions that the high priest might know something. He did not think he would not be able to chase down these clues on this particular trip, and with the turmoil in the area, it probably wouldn't be safe to travel there.

The pilot put the "seat belt" light on, and attendants gathered up the food trays and asked the passengers to buckle up and put their seats up.

Wooosh! Drinks, loose papers, and passengers flew up and dropped just as quickly. The pilot came on with the announcement, "Ladies and Gentlemen, we have just hit an air pocket. We will make the rest of this trip with the seatbelt sign on. Sorry for any inconveniences." James' paper and books flew out of the seat and scattered onto the floor, but with help from the passengers all around, he was able to gather them up again. Unsettled, other passengers were calling on the flight attendants to soothe their fears. James resumed concentrating on the material before him, oblivious to the tension around him.

In his research so far, Professor James had come to the conclusion that whatever was in this scroll Hezron carried was valuable enough to be mentioned by all who came in contact with him. Hezron was a little-known fellow whose only claim to fame was the scroll he rescued out of the Alexandria Library fire. In scores of documents, James' curiosity grew and now was the reason for this entire research project.

Everyone in the archeological world knew of the Professor's obsession, and he was blessed to be contacted by other archeologists and their enthusiasts if they ran across anything remotely mentioning Hezron. Many of his leads came from such sources, and while some were able to photograph, copy, or write down what they had found and acquired for him, some documents were so fragile that no photographs of them were allowed.

In fact, they were so protective of said documents even a viewing had to be arranged years in advance. It was one of the reasons for the time of this trip. Such was the case with parchment at a Paris library to which he was going to check out first. He was indeed fortunate to have been given this opportunity. He wondered about some of the new red light or night vision photography and if it could be used if he found the parchment to be vital to his research project.

The food he had eaten was now making him drowsy, and not long afterward, papers slipped from his fingers, and gentle *zzzzz*'s filled the air. With a soft smile on her face, the flight attendant gathered his stuff, placing them on the seat beside him. She reached up and brought down a pillow and blanket from the upper compartment and, like a mother hen, tucked him in.

The next thing James knew, through the intercom, interrupts, the pilot was informing everyone of the imminent arrival at Paris' Charles de Gaulle International Airport, the weather conditions, and ended with "Thank you for flying American Airlines. We hope you had a pleasant flight. Come fly with us again."

The flight attendants began the final pickups as they did the last checks down the aisles, announcing over the intercom the landing protocols and other disembarking announcements for the passengers. James put the tray table up, gathered up his papers, and stowed them away.

The landing had been uneventful, really smooth, revealing the pilot's experience and care, and in no time was pulling up to the terminal. A flight attendant noticed a slip of paper had fallen from the books but, in the rush of people disembarking, was unable to do anything about it. When the Professor got up to where the flight attendant was, she was able to tell him about the piece of paper he had dropped. He stayed behind her, waiting for the rest of the travelers to disembark so he could go back and retrieve the piece of paper.

When he did get back there, he discovered it was a critical note, now with footprints all over it. In his exuberance of relief at retrieving it, he profusely thanked the flight attendant with hugs and grins. "Thank you, thank you, my itinerary," he said, waving it before her eyes, leaving her a bit ruffled and amused, as he headed out to the concourse. He glanced back down the concourse and, spotting the flight attendant, with the amused smile on her face, waved.

James had arranged a study room at the library in Paris so that he might be able to study the long-awaited moment with the parchment. Grabbing a taxi, he headed over to Bibliotheque' Nationale de France. The intended repository for all writings published in France, the library could trace its origins to the royal library founded at Louvre by Charles V in 1368. A couple of books in the rare section were of interest to him. The library held over 5,000 Greek manuscripts and some rare Hebrew scripts. Pierre, the head librarian, contacted him and subsequently faxed several reference materials, saying besides getting him his appointment for the viewing, he had found 'Hezron' mentioned in a couple of other old documents.

Upon arriving at the Library, Professor Holden looked up at the grand entrance and found himself rather impressed. The library was immense, beautifully laid out, with marble flooring and ornate cathedral ceilings, which he admired as he entered. The librarian, Pierre Travvar, recognized him right away, from the fedora on his head, the bifocals perched on his nose, uncut hair, and now rumpled tweed jacket with patches at the elbows. It was at Professor Johan Goldberg's seminar they had both attended and first met. By mutual interest, they had shared several meals together, discussing the findings and other related subjects of interest.

Pierre hurried over to greet him. Embracing the Professor with a rousing continental-style air kiss on each cheek, Pierre said, "Bon jour, my friend," with more enthusiasm than expected. Shocked and surprised, the Professor quickly recovered from the initial shock of such an intimate display greeting by stepping back to offer his hand.

With a bemused smile, the librarian accepted it and said, "Bon jour, Professor Holden, how good to see you. I believe you have come to check out what I have found in our rare library collection. If you follow me this way, please, I will show you two manuscripts that speak of an educated Jewish traveler named Hezron. It was reported to have one of the manuscripts taken out of the Alexandrian library."

James nodded at Pierre's remarks and, from memory, reviewed some things he knew "When Alexander the Great ruled, he founded the Alexandrian Library in around 300 BC, and it became the repository of all the ancient wisdom and knowledge of that time period. With collectors sent out to all the known world, they gathered and made copies of all the known works of that time. Subsequently, in 415 AD, the library was destroyed along with an estimated half a million books. The total collection was gone in one night, or so we thought. It is such a shame too." James shook his head. "It was said to have had a detailed sun-centered picture of the solar system. It was supposed to have mapped the earth and accurately determined its size. It also reportedly contained the cycle of the precession of equinoxes and a 2160-year cycle of the ages. Such a great loss and tragedy was the Alexandria fire."

"Aww. Yes, that is so true. One of the great losses of all time, truly heartbreaking as any librarian will tell you." Pierre clutched his chest with true Gallic drama. "But what is done is done. Now come follow me." Turning back to the issue at hand, Pierre said, "We must move forward and the reason why you have come here. What I have here is just a brief mention within the context of these manuscripts, and since they are of the right time period, it just might be about the man you are looking for. He has such an unusual name. It would be improbable for there to be many others with the same name." Coming to the right aisle, climbing up the ladder, and pulling two old bound manuscripts, he handed them down to the Professor.

"Wonderful! Thank you. Could I ask you to bring me scrolls numbered 9KLP937 and CK234, please?" James inquired.

Oh, but of course, Professor Holden." "You may call me James," said the Professor.

"Ohhh, but of course, and please call me Pierre," Pierre insisted.

Professor Holden replied with delight on his face, "You remembered our conversation from the seminar, I see," he said, looking in the manuscripts, as Pierre found the notations and showed the Professor.

Pierre laughed and replied, "I have a fondness for the studies of archeology, especially the Middle East. I may not do anything more than read and attend the odd seminar, but I still like to think that if I can contribute to the discovery of some lost find, I will have done my part. You will, of course, mention me in your dissertations if any of what I am about to show you has helped you in your research."

Professor Holden nodded. "Absolutely, and I want to thank you for thinking of me when you ran across this mentioning of Hezron as you have in these manuscripts."

"Now, as to the scrolls you requested, we have an extraordinary place for their viewing. Very fragile, you understand, so please come with me," Pierre said, leading the Professor further into the depths of the immense library.

When they arrived where they were housed, he pointed to a table and chair for James to sit on while he went to get the scrolls requested. He brought out the two ancient scrolls and unrolled them carefully. With careful handling instructions of the scrolls and under the watchful eye of the assistant curator in charge of the rare books, James immediately became engrossed in what was before him.

Knowing his services were needed elsewhere, Pierre bid his adieu, leaving the Professor to dive into the task at hand. James brought out his notebook and wrote furiously, totally absorbed in the information before him. The librarian was proper; this information was another clue to solving the mystery. If what was in these books were accurate, he needed to head over to Alexandria and follow his zig-zag trail to Jerusalem. One of the places mentioned in this document was the same place Professor Goldberg had his dig.

Professor Goldberg was not only an archeologist but a papyrologist. As a papyrologist, he is interested in not only deciphering what was written on any papyri found but in transcribing the ancient languages and reconstructing the fragments found. He especially liked to reconstruct very complex puzzle pieces of papyri found. Components of literature found on rolls of papyrus could extend up to 35 feet in length, and his specialty was not only to unravel them but attach the missing fragments and thus bring to the world great works of literature from the past.

After collecting the information from the scroll, he nodded his head at the assistant curator of rare scrolls, gathered up his papers and returned them to the satchel. Professor Holden headed down to where they kept the maps and was soon outlining his best route to take through the Middle East. He made quick notes of the places he wanted to visit, made copies of areas of particular interest to him, and outlined the best route to include a couple of side stops if he could fit them in.

Pierre Traver, the librarian, soon dropped by to check on him. "Aww. Monsieur Professor, have you found the material to be of interest to your research?"

"Yes, indeed, and now with the help of your maps available here, I can see where he was going and where I must follow," he said, putting photocopies of the maps in his satchel.

"Could I be of any further assistance?" Pierre asked.

"Do you know where Professor Goldberg is now?" he asked, looking over at Pierre, with hope in his eyes.

"Yes, I have continued to keep in contact with him and have his global cell phone number. I find his seminars interesting, and I have always been delighted to take in a seminar or two of his when I get an opportunity. You will find him at the …" Travver looked up at the lights flickering from very bright to dim with an unearthly blue hue. The library building started to shake momentarily, causing his walk to waver and the Professor to grab the table until the shaking stopped.

"Pardon, one moment, please." Nervously he excused himself and swiftly walked away to check into the matter, leaving the Professor staring at his back as he headed down to the first floor.

A little later, when the librarian returned to the front desk, he found the Professor had already found his way to the main lobby. "I must apologize for leaving you so abruptly, but my responsibility is to make sure everything is taken care of. As I was about to say, Professor Goldberg is on an island near Atbara. Here is all the information, including his phone number where he can be reached in the field." Handing James the paper, Pierre again apologized. "My sincere apologies for having to attend another matter, and I wish you well." Just as the Professor turned to leave, Pierre said, "And next time you are in town, maybe we could dine together, as I know of a wonderful place not far from here with exquisite cuisine I would like you to try. A little wine, fine food, and good company are one of the few good pleasures of life. Now I bid you adieu until the next time we meet. Au revoir, my friend."

Professor James said, "No, it is me who should thank you for the kind offers, taking the time to do the research, reserving my appointment to see the rare parchment, and I will gladly take you up on the fine dining the next time I am in Paris. Au revoir, my friend," he said, holding out his overloaded arms to secure a handshake.

While walking out of the library and stopping at the outer atrium, Professor James reached into his satchel for his cell phone. After some fumbling at the bottom of the bag, he pulled it out and called Professor Goldberg. Ensuing conversation confirmed Professor Goldberg was just south of Alexandria. James knew, if the manuscript that he just finished reading was any indication, Professor Goldberg might have a more significant find than even he might realize.

Rain drizzled its last drops as James left the library, leaving the air unsullied and clean. Traffic was thick at this time of the day, and the aroma of French cuisine wafted through the fresh air, causing James' stomach to protest. Checking his watch and calculating his available time, he headed across the street to the café. He placed an order for a beautiful dish of fish and a superb wine suggested by the server to go along with it.

Slowing down was just what the Professor needed; this getting old was getting in the way were his thoughts as he let his body relax in the chair with a sigh. Enjoying the ambivalence and atmosphere brought a smile to his face as he looked around at the beautiful architecture, listened to gentle music floating on the breeze, and the cadence of conversation around him. When the server presented his dinner with a flourish, James first savored the aroma with his eyes closed and a deep sniff. He then openly appreciated the beautiful dish of local fresh trout, puffy pastry, and fresh vegetables in a creamy sauce served with a flare only the French could create. A beautifully breaded trout with hazelnut, herbs, and spices so succulent, he partook with his eyes closed and let his taste buds relish the flavor with every bite. Slowly opening his eyes after savoring such ambrosia of flavor and took a sip of the most excellent wine. *Yes, a pure tantalizing pleasure to be in Paris*, he thought, leaning back in his chair, lifting his glass with a toast, and nodding to the server his approval.

"Nice to take the time to enjoy the atmosphere of the street activities, enjoy the meal, and feel refreshed and ready to move on," he admitted to himself after finishing his meal and getting up after paying. His thoughts were interrupted by a loud protest coming from his left side. He hardly had time to get out onto the street, out of the way of what looked to be an ensuing fight.

BOOM….the restaurant blew, sending him, along with tables and chairs, shrapnel, pieces of the restaurant building, and other patrons flying through the air.

Screams filled the air. People were picking themselves up from the wreckage, helping others still caught in the rubble. With scarves and tearing of t-shirts, good citizens were helping their fellow injured. Sirens were soon adding to the crescendo of intense trauma sounds as the dust settled.

James was fortunate, he may have been thrown, but he was relatively unhurt, except for a few bumps and bruises from landing on a car hood. With the ringing in the ears, James shook his head, brushed himself off, and checked for injuries. Quickly the area was filled with the sounds of police and ambulance sirens and the wounded crying.

James watched the surreal view in front of him. It was like he was watching some disaster movie, and at that moment realized it was real. Knowing he would be caught up in all the ramifications of being a victim, he decided that did not fit in with his plans. The place was busy filling up with fire trucks, police cars, and medical personnel in ambulances coming to attend to the wounded. The ensuing rush by onlookers and emergency personnel to the scene added to the commotion. The injured were being taken away, and police were now starting to go around questioning everyone.

James decided he was not going to get caught up in this mess. Quietly gathering up his satchel with papers intact, James headed down the street and, luckily, in confusion, was overlooked by the officials. Within a few blocks, James relaxed enough to start looking for a taxi.

Flagging down a cab, he headed to the airport to change his flight plans. A short time later, he was at the ticket counter at the airport, getting a change of flight, and unbeknownst to him, he was spotted.

Chapter 3

Two weeks earlier, Sam received a phone call from the Museum of Jewish History's head curator, and a meeting was arranged at four o'clock this afternoon. Sam's reputation must have proceeded him, he thought as he wondered why his firm was chosen and for what reason. Since none was given at the time the appointment was set up, even with consistent questioning throughout the conversation over the phone with the curator, Sam couldn't resist answering with an affirmative for the meet. It was very abnormal for Sam to not follow procedures, and it was his established way of handling everything. He liked to know why they needed him or at least what the meeting was about before going in. Going into any situation blind was not something he did.

Police departments and other government agencies were restricted from becoming involved in civil investigations. Often a private investigator, like his firm, assisted people with evidence that helped with a case or finding someone. Every once in a while, they were called in to gather information or do research on individuals for corporate use.

So what could a curator want? Since it was one of his best client's referrals, and later with a phone recommendation, Sam relented on bending the policy this once, just to talk to the curator. Sam was a by-the-book kind of guy, and Karen, his partner, was the one who worked and managed the gray areas, which took more finesse than he possessed. And in all cases, Sam made sure that they understood and signed their policy that the purchaser would be liable if the information gathered was used unlawfully or illegally. Got to cover one's own butt first was Sam's policy.

Calling his partner, Karen, into his office, Sam brought her up to speed. "I will be over at the curator's office to hear him out on what he might be asking us to do for him. Could you see the connection between John Hodgkins, who referred us, and the curator?"

Karen said, "I already did and did not find anything other than John Hodgkins is a major donor for the museum."

Karen Spangles had been with the company since retiring after an injury she suffered while working as a CIA agent. She had first met Sam on a case in New York that involved some pretty malicious drug cartel operators, and the coordinated effort of the local FBI and CIA agency went a long way toward getting a handle on the case. They met and were assigned to work on the case together, which lasted for nearly six months. She liked working with him, and the progress they made together went smoothly. Sam thought so, too, or he would not have suggested the partnership. She could remember it as if it was yesterday; she thought back to when he asked, "If you ever planned on retiring to civil life, would you be interested in partnering with me and opening a private investigation firm." Not long after that, in another case, Karen was shot in the line of duty and was pensioned off. She contacted Sam and asked him, "when do you plan on opening the private eye business and the rest, as some say, is history. Karen threw her chips in with his and now was the administrative and researching partner while he was the field agent for the firm. She was better at the background investigative work that kept her in the office.

Karen and Sam had been in business for over five years, building a solid reputation in the community. They worked well together and enjoyed each other's company.

Sam came sweeping into the room with his usual bull in a china shop approach, the door flying open, and the rush of thoughts poured out of his mind and unto Karen's lap. It was the approach Karen loved to watch. But it seemed like Sam never saw her, at least not how she would have liked him too. So she stayed focused on business with Sam.

Sam gathering up his contracts and stuffing them into the briefcase, said, "I just got off the phone with a Mr. Bloomberg, curator for the prestigious Museum of Jewish Heritage, and confirmed our meeting. It looks like we have a new case; I will be heading over there right away to meet with him to discuss the details. Could I get you to check into Mr. Bloomberg and find out all you can? Rather curious why a curator would need our services."

Karen making a note of the name on a piece of paper and, turning to Sam, remarked, "Maybe he has lost his mummy from the new 'Egyptian culture, and the Jewish slave 'display they are advertising will be on exhibit next month." Karen always wondered why Sam would leave everything to the last moment before starting. She could have been looking into this case when he knew about it. At least some preliminary work on the client, like background checks, could be done more leisurely. It was one of the bad habits she had not been able to get Sam to refrain from doing.

Sam laughed and said, "Now that would be an appealing case. I could read the headlines now, 'Private eye helps museum solve the mystery of the missing mummy,'" Karen chuckled. Today Karen was not going to bring up her pet peeve because today, she thought it would sound like a nagging wife.

Karen was Sam's partner since the beginning and was invaluable to the compiling and research because of the access to information regarding any project they handled. Being fast and efficient allows Sam to do the fieldwork. The vital intel she armed him with helped their organization become established in the private eye work as one of the city's most professional, proficient, confidential, influential private investigative firms. She had worked for the CIA for years and, with her connections, was an invaluable resource. Sam truly loved Karen but never figured out a way of approaching her.

His background with the Marines and later the FBI helped make their company's clientele almost exclusively high-level contract work. Right now, his business was experiencing a lull. Since the curator indicated one of their clients had referred their company, he thought it was prudent to do the curator a favor for the sake of his more critical client and see if he could be of service.

Walking into the curator's office, private investigator Sam Piece glanced around the room, taking in the collections, the degrees on the wall, the books on the shelf, and the spacious desk neatness. He wanted to learn as much about the man, his passions, tastes, and interests as unobtrusively as possible, still a little more than curious as to why a curator of the Museum of Jewish Heritage would have a need to hire his firm. He and his partner, Karen, had built up an outstanding reputation for being able to handle the strangest of cases, but to have a museum needing his help was a stretch of even his imagination.

He was greeted by a well-groomed gentleman, who introduced himself, "Hello, I am going to assume you are the private eye I have scheduled to meet with." Sam nodded, so the curator continued, "As Head Curator and Anthropologist of Middle Eastern History, I am Mr. Bloomberg." Mr. Bloomberg extended his hand and gestured towards a chair with the other. "Welcome, Mr. Pearce; so glad you could come. Would you care for anything to drink," he asked about going to the small beverage bar.

Sam shook his head, thus preventing him from proceeding further and catching his attention so he could look directly into the curator's eyes. "Well, thank you for the offer, but no, thank you, although I must admit I am inquisitive as to why you would need our services."

Mr. Bloomberg willingly explained, "Our Museum is currently focusing on the nineteenth and twentieth century's artifacts of Jewish history for display; in addition to the current display, our Museum does collect and study all aspects of the history of Jews. I am always looking to expand the culture, historical, and religious history of the Jews. We include books, clothing, artwork, and religious objects. Have you ever taken a tour of our Museum?" Mr. Bloomberg now watched Sam for any indication of knowledge or interest in the Jewish Heritage.

Sam sadly nodded, "No, I am afraid not." And the answer seemed to please the curator in some strange way, which puzzled Sam. So the curator was glad he didn't know much. So he wants me to work without background knowledge or, as one would say, in the dark.

The curator continued, "Well, I suppose we should get to the reason I am recruiting your firm. As I explained over the phone, you have come highly recommended, and I will get right to the point. There was a lead on a significant artifact the Museum is seriously interested in procuring, and James Holden, a professor, will soon be heading out of the country in pursuit of this artifact if my sources are correct. So I will get right to the point. We wish to procure your services to follow the Professor no matter where in the world he goes and report to us any and all of his activities."

Sam asked, "Do you have any more details?"

Mr. Bloomberg shook his head. "I wouldn't worry about the details; all you have to do is tail the Professor and report all activities. You might want to track his son down as he is assisting his father on this one. His name is John Holden, a student here at a local university. My main focus would be on the Professor, though. If and when the Professor finds the artifact he is looking for, I would appreciate you procuring it from him." Sam was given documents the curator had gathered on the Holden. The curator said, "I do have an extraction team ready to expedite all matters regarding the artifact."

In the back of Sam's mind, he wondered just how valuable this artifact was, to have an extraction team already in place, and just how far they were willing to go. But his training shut down any further lines of thought along that direction, for he was clearly in the 'need to know' division. He had a funny feeling he needed to know, not so much about the artifact in question but who was behind this demand. Another question ran through his mind if the curator had an extraction team already in place, why not use them to do the investigation too?

Sam shrugged and said, "Sounds easy enough, but I just have to ask, 'why don't you work directly with the Professor?'"

The curator paused a moment as a rather grim face came across his features," The Professor and the university he works for are affiliated with another organization. We believe this is not a good place for such an artifact. We have a serious concern, should this artifact actually be uncovered and by chance found in the Islamic world, there is an excellent probability that the jihad fanatics will make a concerted effort to destroy it. Security becomes paramount with this rare piece."

Sam nodded with an affirmation of understanding, "And we can't have it destroyed, so that is where I come in. Is the extraction team not able to do the investigation?"

"No, they do not have the resources that your company has to track someone. And," the curator added, "we have talked with the Middle Eastern government officials, and they are not willing to talk or negotiate any deal over something that has yet to materialize. So that leaves us no choice but to take matters into our own hands."

Sam raises one eyebrow. "Taking matters into your own hands?"

Mr. Bloomberg shrugged. "Let's just say, in this situation, anyone on the trail of this artifact would be under investigation, just in case it turns up," and with a shuffle of papers moved the conversation on with, "but I have said enough. Just be prepared to do whatever it takes to get the artifact, should it be found before the Professor has a chance to really study it if that is possible. Is that understood?"

"Yes, sir," Sam said before realizing his military training response was out of place.

"If and when the Professor finds the artifact, call me immediately so that I may determine whether it is the article in question." Mr. Bloomberg continued with his thoughts without regard to Sam's gaffe.

Sam raised both of his eyebrows this time at the commanding sound of the curator's voice on the word 'immediately' but nodded and produced his contract papers for the curator to sign.

The natural light shining through the window started to dance in colors across the room, causing both men to move over to the window to see why. The northern lights were dancing above the New York skyline, reflecting off of buildings and windows in a soft glow of subtle rainbow hues along with the evening sunset. They swirled from the east to the west in a beautiful array of arcs of blue; one bright pick hue burst up from the north like tongue-licking cotton candy. They rippled across the skies in all their glory, and Sam wished he had brought his camera to capture it all on film; it was so beautiful. The colors kept changing, sometimes from a deep red color to purple as the solar winds hit different gases. They both stood in fascination with this spectacular phenomenon, the beauty in the auroras as they flew over their heads. Too soon, the show was over. Sam acknowledged, "Now that was different," as he looked around him in bewilderment.

To which the curator replied, "Yes, strange indeed but very beautiful," still looking out the window to see if there were any more coming.

Sam returned to the desk to gather his papers and shake hands with the curator. After leaving the curator's office with a new case and a nice advance, Sam dialed Karen's number upon leaving the building. He turned the ignition on in his car, clearing left, and pulled out into what earlier had been light traffic while the phone rang. It looked like it was going to be slow going all the way back to the office, for the traffic had definitely picked up.

Karen answered the phone with the customary greeting, "S and K Private Investigators, how may I ….help you?" but Sam interrupted her mid-sentence.

"Sam here. What have you found out so far?" he said, busily negotiating a change of lanes.

Karen grabbed her note papers, as she had already started the investigational groundwork on the curator and the Museum. Karen, putting the glasses back up on her nose, read aloud, "Mr. Bloomberg, born on the west coast, raised by his mother, showed an intense interest in history since high school, where all his top scores were. In college, he studied history and graduated Sum Cum Laude in Library Science, majoring in Archival Science. He received a degree of distinction for his research thesis on museology. The curator has been with the Museum for over ten years now. After graduation, he had a stint in Jerusalem as a volunteer worker with the archivist at the Israel Museum. He has an outstanding record of research papers on the subjects of the process of overseeing, arranging, cataloging, and exhibiting collections. He is currently single with no evidence of ever being married except to his job as far as I can tell." Karen looked up and teasingly asked, "Maybe he is my type?"

"Naahhhh," Sam fired back.

"Killjoy," she retorted. "As far as I know, he has been a valuable asset to the Museum since he was hired. He turned into a very viable entity in the community," she said, flipping through her papers to ensure that she had reported everything she had gathered so far.

"And that was about all I could find so far" leaning back in her chair, she stretched some of the tight muscles in her neck. Working at the computer always tightened up between her shoulders.

But Sam wanted more, so he asked, "Could you check out those he might be associating with also?"

"Ok," Karen said as she made notes, "I will see what I can come up with. But what should I be looking for?"

"I will tell you when I get to the office," he said as he turned left, throwing the briefcase in the back of the car before it tumbled from the passenger seat to the floor. . Sam told Karen, "I will be there shortly."

Arriving at the office, Sam started picking Karen's brain. "All the curator said doesn't add up as a legitimate request. Why would the curator want to pay for our expenses on this wild goose chase on a perchance it may or may not even materialize? What is it so important that even a hint of a lead is enough to get us involved? What really gets me is that I am asked to whisk away said article, and I am not a thief. You, on the other hand, who did a lot more gray area covert operations, can probably see and understand the need better than I."

Karen interrupts with, "Yeah, we, CIA operatives, sometimes did work the gray areas for the good of our country, and this might be just that simple. The curator is doing what is necessary for the prosperity and preservation of Jewish history."

Sam just wasn't made that way and outlined where he may cut and run in this case, "I am only letting you know, just so that you do understand where I may draw the line on this case," and as an afterthought, added, "only time will tell. We will be reporting to him as we are paid to do for now."

Rubbing his fingers across his forehead, Sam felt the need to explain himself. "You see, I found it really interesting that our dear little curator already has an 'extraction team, 'and that is why I have asked you to check out those he associates with. We may not want to be involved with his 'extraction team.' We may be on the 'need to know the basis on this one, but I say we need to know more about this 'extraction team,' and anyone who is pressuring the curator to do this," Sam said with distaste in his mouth. "I just don't like the 'before the Professor even has a chance to examine it, if possible,' and I am quoting the curator's words here. And he wanted me to make sure I got that last part, which is where all my red flags went up on this curator."

"It could be nothing more than some of the special efforts that those in his line of work do," Karen suggested. "Besides, this is just a job, we get paid to do this, and so that is what we do," she said in the voice of practicality.

Sam bobbed his head as he mulled over Karen's perspective." True, he is taking on his shoulders the issues of international laws regarding the acquisitions and transportation of antiquities, which is in addition to dealing with the current local rules of this country should this thing be found. I can't help it, and I just keep getting the feeling that there is something fishy about it," he said, scowling. He was going to proceed with caution.

Karen said, "Since we aren't in the business to question but to gather the information as per client request, which is simple enough and with the kind of pay offered, which you did accept along with the assignment, I would say that we are committed. You worry too much, and nothing may come of this. So don't delve too deeply into this, and thus you will be able to walk away without knowing much and a clear conscience," she offered, hoping to reassure her partner.

Sam knew that many things are done in the gray area of the law. He informed Karen, "I will be reporting all movements of the Professor directly to the curator. But I will also keep you posted on this. You always have a way to help me see clearly a way through some of these shady areas of ethical issues I may be dealing with." Sam justified himself and acknowledged Karen's approach. As far as he could foresee, and with a bit of self-reassurance that the activities of one lone Professor should be all on the up and up and nothing too out of the ordinary, he finally let the worrying thought go.

After more computer investigation, Karen informed Sam, "While the information of the curator was scant, I have just run across some records that he was at Harvard for a semester, changed majors from Law to Archeology. He accepted this position as a favor to the family," she said, looking up at Sam. "It seems that Mr. Bloomberg is well connected and comes from a wealthy orthodox Jewish family."

And with that, Karen said, "Listen, I need to get back to work and see what else I can dig up," turning back to the computer, thus blocking out any further conversation.

"Keep digging," Sam said as he turned to his desk, hoping to learn more. Shifting his shoulders and putting his feet up on his desk, he rearranged his mind to settle in on the case before him. Spying on Professor James Holden, just to observe and report his activities until told otherwise, Sam thought about gathering up all the information files currently collected on his desk. Digging into the documents and photo he was given on James, which gave him a starting point, he took a sip of coffee Karen always kept warm and ready on his desk.

Karen, on the phone, briefly turned to him, already back with more information. "James Holden's credit card activity has recently shown up as being active in Paris." Sam threw his files into his briefcase and headed out the door, saying, "Call a cab, hold down the fort until I get back. It looks like I am going to Paris."

Calling the curator on the private number he was given, he said, "Professor James Holden is in Paris," without any preamble.

Mr. Bloomberg said, "Get on the next plane and do not worry about the expenses!"

"Already heading there now," Sam said as he continued down the flight of stairs and out of the building. It was a good thing Sam always kept a suitcase in the trunk of his car packed for such an event. Traveling on short notice does happen in his business, and he always made it a point to be prepared. Getting the luggage out of the car just after the taxi arrived made him smile. It was excellent to see it come; rare for New York Cab companies to respond so quickly. Getting in the cab, he directed the cabby to take him to the bank first and then to the airport.

Right after he got off the phone with Bloomberg, Sam gets back on with Karen to report his latest information. "I spoke with the curator, and he said to go to Paris. I will be in touch." The static on the phone was terrible, and it did not seem to be the bars; Sam listened harder and had to repeat and ask Karen to repeat herself too. This was strange. Both of them had satellite phones, and there were very few places where they did not have good connections. Sam was puzzled and wondered if he had damaged his phone somehow. The reception finally cleared up, and they were able to finish their conversation. Karen ended the conversation with, "Talk to you when you touch down in Paris."

"Will do," he said and hung up as he purchased his tickets at the airport counter. Sam was fortunate to get a standby seat on the next flight out to Paris.

Sam, upon disembarking, found his phone ringing, and Karen, on the other end, said without much adieu. "He just upgraded his ticket with Egyptian Airlines flight 3546 seat 34B out of Paris to Cairo."

"Thanks," Sam said, shutting the phone and immediately heading towards the ticket counter, just in time to spot James picking up his satchel to move on. Sam moved into line and was able to obtain the only available seat left, and just his luck, it was the window seat beside the Professor.

Giving Karen a quick call, he said, "Guess what, I have the only remaining seat on Professor Holden's flight. You are not going to believe this. My seat is next to him, and I need a good cover story."

Karen thought for a moment. "Do you remember your stint in China where you were working for the border brokerage firm, spying on its rival?"

"Yeah," Sam said.

Thinking quickly, Karen said, "Well, do you remember enough so you could pass as one of their men in the sales management division?"

Sam was catching her drift. "Hey, I can do it. I think it will work. Thanks. Got to go," he said, hanging up as he ran to catch his flight when he heard the last call for his flight over the intercom.

Immediately after hanging up the phone, Mr. Bloomberg closed the door to his office and made a call. Speaking in low tones into the phone, he reported the essential parts of what the investigator told him. Nodding his head, confirming the investigator is following Holden. After remarking on how the Museum would definitely be in the loop when it came time, he smiled as he hung up the phone.

Thinking things were going to turn out better than he thought. He immediately went to work on a presentation for the Egyptian artifacts, which would be on display all next month. If he remembered right, Susan Channing might know something. She works down in the back but had volunteered last year to work during her vacation time on an archeology site with Professor Campbell somewhere in the Middle East. It wouldn't hurt to see what period they were uncovering.

The curator knew the influence of Hezron extended far beyond Jewish circles. There was even an apocryphal letter of the so-called "Preston," which appeared in some religious circles and asserted the existence of independent Jewish states, contrary to some authorities. Crusades had done their best to remove all traces of the tribes over the years, and the last thing that needs to surface is more proof of their existence.

Returning his mind to work at hand, he headed to the back to talk with Susan. As he turned the corner, he saw her bent over an artifact she was cleaning up for display. Picking up the piece, she gracefully moved with the lithe moves of a gazelle, graceful and fluid, spellbinding. He was rooted to his spot until she had the artifact on the table. She had always been one of his finest workers. Articulate, efficient, very methodical, and detail orientated, she was his number one associate on his preservation team.

Susan was young for her accomplishments, and with a youthful air about her, she tossed her long hair back out of the way as she continued to clean the article on the table, using a magnifying glass for the detail. She was boyish-looking yet did have a specific feline attribute that clearly showed up when she looked at men. Susan might be all brains, but there was nothing to deny her appeal. And she knew it. Right now, he knew she had set her eyes on him, and it was the one snag in the working relationship really bothering him. He hesitated in his approach with a slight frown as the thought crossed his mind. He may one day have to deal with her sexual banter that always remained under the wire and left tension in the air.

With the most authoritative voice he could muster, He called attention to his presence with a, "Ha hmm," and she giggled as if she had known all along he was there. It was always disconcerting for him to be in her presence. He felt like she was reading his mind and found it amusing, which is not playing fair in any relationship. He decided to go straight to the point. "Could I have your attention for a moment, please?" he said with as much authority as he politely could muster.

She slowly put down her tools and wiped her hands, all the while smiling a feline smile, which seemed to be saying she knew more than he did. She turned her piercing eyes upon him and murmured, "You have my complete attention. How can I be of assistance, Director?" she said, purring the last word.

"If I remember right, you were on an archeological dig in the Middle East last year. I was wondering if there was anything relating to Jewish history in that particular dig?" Mr. Bloomberg stated with his back straight and a no-nonsense expression on his face.

Smiling softly, she said, "No, nothing I can recall. Is there anything else?" Leaving the air to hang heavy with the question.

"No! No, that will be all. Thank you. "And with that, Mr. Bloomberg did an about-face, hoping that he had turned before his cheeks became so inflamed that he would die of embarrassment. She was so disconcerting!

She quietly turned back to her work, picked up her tools, and resumed cleaning the artifact she had been working on, smiling to herself like his presence had amused her. She knew the attraction between them scared him more than he would ever admit, and it amused her as she was in no rush to enter into a relationship with him until he wanted it.

He just didn't know how to handle her and wished she was not so accomplished or so good at her work. It was disconcerting to be in her presence, and he didn't know what to do about it. Mumbling to himself, he quickly retreated back to his office, feeling inept at dealing with her presence.

Chapter 4

Two days earlier, Travis packed up his bags and papers and attempted to get advanced tickets for New York, but none were available, so he waited at the airport on standby. He had never done standby before, and to be at the mercy of the system for a ride, he thought, was crazy. He had two purposes for going, one was to attend a consortium under the direction of Professor Tom Pagett from the Colgate University in Hamilton, New York, at the Department of Physics and Astronomy, and the other was to deliver a package.

Travis was in the understudy program at the Observatory in Hawaii as an assistant to Professor Jordon. He had come to New York to attend the Consortium for lunar influences on near objects. Travis was now in his last year of the undergraduate study program, and now with more time to finish his doctorate thesis, he attended more seminars and postgraduate consortiums to help further his work. Travis's Professor had given him the package to drop off. It provided an excuse to meet Professor Pagett, whom Professor Jordon believed would be of great help to his protégé in his doctoral thesis, as Professor Pagett was one of the renowned authorities on near objects.

After the lecture, Travis worked his way through the crowd to approach Professor Pagett. With the package in hand. "Professor, Professor Pagett, may I have a moment of your time, please?" Travis called out as the Professor was heading out the side door.

The Professor turned as Travis pushed his way against the throng heading out of the back of the auditorium. He paused and waited until the young fellow reached him before asking, "How may I help you?"

Travis gathered his breath and said, "Professor Jordon, from the Hawaii Observatory, gave me this package as I was coming to New York anyway to attend your lecture." He says, 'you asked for these to be brought to you ASAP.'"

Professor Pagett's eyes lit up, and he took the package from the rugged young man and asked, "How much do you know about my work and what is in the package?"

Travis smiled and said, "A bit. I am one of your greatest admirers, especially your work on the X366. I am especially interested in the near object X366 scheduled to arrive in 2022, and I am doing undergraduate work in near objects as my thesis."

Bringing out his hand to shake, he said, "I am Travis O'Reilly, a student under Dr. Jordon."

Professor Pagett nodded and, shaking his hand, said, "Travis O'Reilly, so you are the one Dave, I mean Professor Jordon, told me so much about. He has high hopes for you and your work. Now, as far as near object X366, we have made some revisions ever since. In fact, just in from NASA, this object is so far pointing directly at us; NASA has not been able to calculate its arrival as we first thought. Back in 1997, we thought it would be around 2035, and by 2000 we soon realized it was coming in a lot faster rate than the estimated 2022 you mentioned."

Travis, taken back a little bit, frowned and asked, "Well, just how soon do you think it will arrive?"

The Professor said, "That is where what you have brought me might just have the answer to your question. Whatever the answer, the public will not hear of this as it has been given a top-secret status, and now even I am not allowed privy to what NASA knows, so I can't tell you much more. I was hoping to get on the study panel, but I could not get the clearance necessary. I, unfortunately, was out of the loop. Besides, if the government knows it will be heading directly for the earth and large enough to lay waste to what we know as earth, I don't know if the public will hear anything more, except those directly involved with the panel."

Travis shrugged. "Sorry to hear they didn't want you involved in the study panel. I would definitely be interested in what you do know."

Professor Pagett smiled and, with a conspirator's wink, said, "I will try to get as much information as I can when I can, as this fascinates me. I believe what is in your packet is what Professor Jordon said over the phone would surprise me. I have been calculating based on the information we have had so far, and it looks like it might arrive around 2014 or 2015, but do not quote me on this. Just keep it under your hat, and hopefully, we will start hearing more about this as the day approaches."

Travis's mind started calculating his chances the Professor could squeeze him in, "Is there any chance I may go with you and see what the Professor has provided, and maybe help with the calculations? After all, it is what my dissertation is on, and it would really help me for my doctorate. I hope it will validate all that I have written so far."

Professor Pagett turned and started to head out the door, with Travis by his side. "Sure, follow me." Now leaving the building and heading towards his car, he said, "So far, as I understand, it is on target. Fact, NASA has been commissioned to blow up near objects, and they blew up one in 2006, which they were very successful at without much public knowledge. So I am figuring they are gearing up for the big one, but you are welcome to my home tonight, where we can continue this conversation. By that time, I will have a little time to read what is in the packet and see if relevant."

"That would be fantastic!" Travis exuberantly declared, grinning.

"Why not come with me now as I am done for the day? That is, if you have nothing better to do? And since you are not my student, why don't I call you by your first name and you do the same for me. I hate formality. By the way, call me Tom," he said, putting his arm out to push the exit door open.

With a smile, Travis said, "Ok, Tom," and the two headed to the car, talking about mutual friends. Professor Pagett's car was a remarkably well-preserved aged Volvo that had seen better days, Travis thought as they piled into the vehicle. He was beginning to wonder if they would even make it to the Professor's house, and transportation was not on the top of the man's list of priorities.

They were soon at the Professor's Tudor manor, where the older man led Travis to his study. He pulled up the portable chalkboard where one side was already full of notations and, flipping it over, revealed a maze of calculations. Travis studied it while the Professor opened up the package, went over the pictures and the documentation, and was soon back at the chalkboard. Flipping the chalkboard over, the Professor was quickly mapping out the latest sightings with the last known. Together, with the latest information, they worked on the new triangulation. Configuring the speed, weight, and size of the near object, they determined the trajectory and impact location on earth of this near earth object imminent.

So engrossed they were that they completely forgot about food until the wee hours. They took a break to raid the refrigerator and review their information and work. Travis sighed, "I wish I could use the computer at the observatory, which is already preprogrammed to calculate all we have just finished. Do you realize that what has taken us six hours would have taken a matter of a few minutes for the computer program SC5?"

Tom shrugged. "I am used to the old fashion way, and it gives me time to validate the reasons for each calculation. I bet you have not done hand calculations in a long time?"

Travis laughed. "No kidding, I am of the computer generation, where everything is on the computer, and I can't live without it. You amazed me with your understanding of mathematics concerning the near objects' weight, size, and speed. What scares me, though, is, if you are correct, we are in for one hell-of-a hard hit."

Tom soberly nodded. "I figure, if it hits the earth, it could rock it hard, causing earthquakes in so many places, tsunamis in multiple places of the size unheard of, setting off volcanoes spewing ash all over for years to come, and to top it off...." The Professor suddenly dropped his conversation and sandwich back on the counter and moved abruptly back to the study. With a few strokes of the eraser, he removed the last half of the calculation, made appropriate changes, and said, "I think I may know where it will hit, and if it hits there, it could increase the spin of the earth, and we will have shorter days with unheard of wind and weather storms. I am going to head over to the office and have my calculations run through the computer to verify everything."

Tom gathers his papers together. Ultimately he wanted to head down to NASA's "Future Concepts and Transformation Division," armed with ammunition for his inclusion on the panel. While he may not be on the board, they have used him as a consultant, and he did have some good connections to those involved in the NIEIPE, the Natural Impact Event Interagency Planning Exercise committee. Their job was to explore the "whole government" response to any impending asteroid strikes.

With this new date and location of impact, they could better focus on the disaster response and deflection or mitigate the asteroid impact. "Impact accuracy is of utmost importance, you know," Tom said, acknowledging Travis's presence with this comment. Checking the time, he picked up the phone and called to see if Paul was available to speak.

Holding his hand over the phone, he turned to Travis and asked, "Is it ok if you see yourself out. I'll be leaving shortly, right after making this call. I need to make this call right now while the information is fresh in my mind. Been good working with you; tell Dave his protégé is just as he said he would be. Glad to have made your acquaintance and would love to work with you in the future. You can use me as a reference if you need one."

"Appreciate it, and thanks; I enjoyed working with you too." Travis nodded and, with a wavelet, himself out the door while Professor Pagett watched him go.

Turning back to the phone, Tom Pagett waited for Paul, who worked for NASA, to get on the line. Paul was his fellow Professor at the University before he took on this new position with NASA. Knowing the procedures used or adapted, new and needs to be elevated to higher level exercises with more senior partners. He was hoping that with proper planning and response from the NEO emergency team, the required delineation of organizational responsibilities would not tangle up the notifications and protocols of dealing with the volume of affirmative action required.

In his mind, it meant he should be required to come on board and lead a team of experts on this project. Not going to happen.

This bureaucracy was riddled with the current program policies, and the Professor was afraid it would not work efficiently during a crisis. His lack of faith in the system went back many years, and he had a sneaky suspicion it was one of the reasons he was not chosen.

One of the good things about NEO was the NEO detection community's work openly using Internet communications and web-based data sets. Very likely, the information of any new discovery of high interest would be made available to the public. The disadvantage is it is before NASA can completely and adequately validate the possible impact. Another disadvantage in providing fodder for their news releases was accuracy, reliability, and, ultimately, credibility for those reporting. Openly using the internet communications and web-based data sets is a gold mine for rumor-mongers and conspiracy theorists, which Professor Pagett cringed over when it came to his reputation. He believed the opportunity to notify other appropriate agencies needed to go first.

He decided that he would save the actual reporting to NEO if other avenues meaning his appointment for the heading of this project, remained closed to him. Public safety and tranquility required that the federal government be able to rapidly establish a single authoritative voice and the tools to present any critical information. It was the Professor's understanding that, for this reason, it was best to not post this through NEO. Leaving a message on Paul's answering service to call back, the Professor went back to gathering up his papers and getting ready to head to another lecture scheduled.

Travis returned to his hotel to change, get cleaned up, and get some badly needed rest. Falling on the bed, he was soon asleep on top of the covers. It was late afternoon when Travis woke up, starving. He cleaned up and headed out to find something to eat.

Since he was in the city of New York, he decided to take in the sites and found the area full of ethnic foods and restaurants, filling the air with tantalizing smells and making his mouth water as he strolled down the street. He chose a fantastic Italian restaurant and afterward found himself caught up in the New York nightlife. Visiting one of the night spots on the west side, he soon found himself enjoying an evening of dancing with a beautiful young lady, and it wasn't until the wee hours before he came out and started looking for a cab.

Hearing a noise, he stopped and turned towards the sound. Looking out towards the alley, where the shuffling and scuffling noises he heard were coming from, he noticed two men battling it out. He listened to the sound of a gun going off, and one man crumpled to the ground. Shocked, Travis found himself frozen still, unable to believe what he had just witnessed. The man left standing looked his way, and Travis got a perfect look at his face. The killer called out to his buddies who were outside of Travis' vision as he bolted in Travis's direction.

Travis clearly outnumbered, fled down the street, pursued by three men, who fired a couple of shots at him. He had never been so scared in his life. If it wasn't for this place he had broken into and now hiding in, he believed he would be dead by now.

Chapter 5

The terminal at the airport had more than the usual amount of travelers, congesting the counters and rescheduling their flights. After a long wait, Professor James could change his airline ticket and boarded another plane for Cairo as it was leaving sooner. Sam was one of the last to arrive on the airplane, just catching it before the flight attendant was about to close the door. James was stowing away his backpack, as were other passengers making the last-minute preparations for the flight. The passenger in front of Sam was an elderly doddering lady who took forever, bottling up the aisle, and if it wasn't for Sam's help with the overhead compartment, he might still be standing while the plane took off. The seats were rapidly filling up, and it looked like it was going to be very full this flight. By the time he got to his seat, Professor James was comfortably seated with his satchel of papers lying in Sam's window seat.

Walking boldly up to Professor James' seat, he stowed his carry-on above, "Could I have you move your papers? This is my seat," he said before saying, "excuse me," to James and squeezing his mighty frame past James' knees and into the window seat.

Sam asked, "Is this your first trip to Egypt?" once he got himself comfortable, trying to think of an excellent way to get the conversation started.

James shook his head. "No, not my first and probably will not be my last.

"James thought this man was a friendly enough seat companion. It is always good to meet another American in these foreign countries, especially on a long flight.

Sam introduced himself. "My name is Sam Hatcher, by the way, and I am in sales. My company, KHN, just promoted me to the overseas sales division, which I am really excited about. An opportunity to show my company what I can do and validate that they had made the right choice," Sam said while holding out his hand with a charming smile on his face.

Upon shaking Sam's hand, James asked, "Well, hello Sam, I am James. What exactly does KHN sell?"

Sam said, "We are a commodities international brokerage and cross-border customs brokerage firm. Our company has many locations around the world. This is my first assignment, with my new promotion, to open up the Egyptian branch.

"Well, congratulations on the promotion. So what is on the agenda for this trip for you?" James asked.

"I am to do some research into the country's market and what I call to get a taste of the bordering countries that we will be doing business with and are considering branching out to." Sam, acting like he was eager to add another client to his list, yammered on like he was the best broker in the business. "Our commodity traders can trade by phone, email, or online website by using one of our state-of-the-art trading platforms that quickly routes your orders to the filling broker in the pits. Our company provides the highest level of service for all its customers and their needs. We have the best possible rates and the most up-to-date research and trading tools to assist anyone trading across international lines. We understand all this and have dedicated ourselves to providing the very best for our customers," he said and handed James his business card. "Contact me and find out what we have to offer that meets your needs. If you are into the international trade of commodities and need assistance getting your supplies in or out of a country, we are here for you in executing your plans or helping you establish a plan. Whatever it takes to meet our customer's needs. Our motto is 'Across the world, we are there opening all border gates for you.'"

James asked, "Is your company involved in transporting goods out of the country?"

Sam said, "Yes, numerous people are either affiliated or enlisted with my company to handle tariffs and other border crossing paperwork as well as the actual transportation of goods. We are one of the leading global border brokerages, providing customs brokerage, freight forwarding, and even warehousing and distribution and shipping services. Our customer-driven solutions make your border crossing shipping, importing, and exporting easier."

James leaned forward and looked intently at Sam, "What about articles that are not for sale but need to be transported? Could your company help me with that?"

Sam leaned back and, with a proper amount of hesitation, asked, "What exactly are we talking about transporting?"

James shrugged. "I am in the archeological field, and if all goes well, I will need to have mechanisms in place to move delicate items smoothly to a secure location."

Sam encourages James to tell more with, "Any details you can give me?"

James shrugged. "Maybe some parchments, if my calculations are correct."

Sam quizzed, "Why can you not use the regular networks within the archeological community for this? I am sure protocols and specialty agents are already in place to handle something this delicate? And sensitive material? Why not use them?"

James acknowledges the wisdom of his question, "We are working with several countries' agencies as we speak, but because of the religious overtones to the material in question, it may not be safe to entrust it in the hands of certain governments in the region. I have a serious concern for its safety."

Sam leaned back and nodded. "If you need help, I just might be able to help."

Now that interested James, for if it was true and the leads were genuine, it follows that Sam may be just the company he should have as a backup so that they could easily take care of the logistics of transportation across borders for him. Usually, the University worked with the local museum on archeology articles. Thus, other countries can place artifacts in a collection on loan for display and study. But with the countries in such turmoil and relationships with the Middle East unpredictable, it might be prudent to have another connection. Right now, being retired, his connection to the University severed; he was at loose ends on what he should do, should actually find something. James took the card Sam offered as he wasn't ready to hear any more spiel from this salesman.

James knew that his University wasn't particularly interested in this study. He had already been turned down for a grant research proposal in conjunction with his offering new class courses in Middle East history, its religion, and related ancient astrological studies. The grant research staff had already reached their quota of investigations with what was ongoing and in the works, and they were not willing, at this time, to allow Professor James to pursue another one. James subsequently requested a sabbatical to pursue this on his own.

For the last fourteen years, James had been reading everything he could on the elusive parchment and all who seemed to know of its existence and the man last known to have it. The University offered him an excellent retirement package instead. Still, it did suggest their post-graduate department program for seminars on the subject should he wish to submit a syllabus with an outline of the curriculum and course content.

There had been many a dead-end trail, years spent in libraries around the world, and seminars on related subjects; Professor James was like a tenacious bulldog and was unwilling to let go of this project. This time James believed that he was getting closer to the answers he had been looking for and maybe actually discovering where Hezron left the scroll. He could feel it in his bones, and with excitement glittering in his tired old eyes, he smiled softly to himself.

"So, what has put you on this plane to Cairo?" Sam asked, hoping to get the Professor started revealing what he knew.

Turning to Sam, James started talking about his favorite subject, "It is actually quite fascinating. It seems that there was a fellow called Hezron who somehow got his hands on a scroll from the Alexandrian library just before the fire burned everything up and later was known as a merchant traveler back in the fourth century. He claimed that he was a citizen of an independent Jewish state somewhere in the eastern region of Egypt."

Sam liked that the Professor was opening up to him and leaning in and giving the man his full undivided attention, encouraged James to continue with an "Uhhh, huh. So what have you gathered so far about this fellow?"

James, now tickled to have an audience for his pet subject, continued with, "A very unique name and the coincidence of both in the same time period, traveling with a scroll is rare indeed. There is a certain way Hebrews dealt with examining and slaughtering animals to see if they were kosher. This particular way of slaughter is only knowingly practiced in the Sudan region. Which is one of the clues that have led me to my current research trip."

"That is a clue? How so?" Sam asked in the hope that it was this piece of information that the curator was after.

"Orthodox Jews have a certain way of making things kosher, and to have another similar but different way declared just as kosher gives evidence to a more ancient way."

As James warmed up to telling his story, his voice picked up the pace. "The way it was told, Hezron was traveling with another man on one of his merchant journeys when a great storm came up on the river as they were crossing it and wrecked the boat. From the journal that Hezron wrote, He gave glory to God for preparing a plank for him and his companion, and they floated on it until they were thrown ashore during this storm. On the shore was an unfriendly tribe called Roman. His companion, who was injured, was immediately killed, and Hezron was put into a pit as a prisoner while they decided whether to kill him or sell him off as a slave. I am not boring you with all these details, am I?"

"No. No! Please continue," Sam declared as he opened his eyes wider and blinked a few times to get the blurred vision out.

"Good. I conjecture that Hezron studied the scroll he stole only when he knew no one was looking in on him and where the light shone on the pit floor as it had to have been dark down there. There is no mention of the scroll or its contents in anything I had uncovered so far when I researched the Roman tribe. The Roman tribe gives no indication of the influence of the scroll on its members, like other tribes Hezron came in contact with. He did indicate he saved the scroll parchment under his tunic close to his chest, valuing it even above his own life. Hezron believes that God has honored him to be the carrier of this document, and it was his divine assignment to return it to the rightful tribe. It seems, from his writings in the journal, the more he read the scroll, the more he was certain God would guide him to the one he was to give it to. In various places within his journal, Hezron kept mentioning the conviction that he was to carry the document to someone of the Melchizedek order," Professor James expounded.

"So, this scroll, Hezron believed to be his divine assignment, is that what you are really after?" Sam asked encouragingly as he fastened his seat belt for the flight.

James nodded but didn't think anything significant about the question as he blithely continued with his tale. "One morning, Hezron must have heard screams and the sounds of struggle and war cries as a neighboring tribe assailed his captors. The surprise attack did not take long if his journal is correct, and soon there was silence."

Sam nodded and observed, "It looks like you are really getting to know this Hezron fellow because you make it sound like you were there with him when you talk about his travels."

"Can't help; I have come to know him pretty well over the last fourteen years. How he wrote it all down in the journals that survived. Hezron recorded how he waited in silence, praying all would be well. Not long before, he was discovered and taken out of the pit. Captured Hezron, along with women, treasures, and livestock, they headed out across the desert on their camels and horses. Everything else they destroyed by burning. They must have run into a traveling caravan of merchants to whom they bargained the women, treasures, and slaves for food and other staple goods because, from what I understand, Hezron was sold. All recorded in his journal," he said, as the plane made a smooth take-off and headed out into the wild blue yonder.

"Ahhh, a man of adventure, I see. You really have come to know a lot about the travels and life of this man," Sam said, getting caught up in the story. The plane was now leveling off at its assigned cruising altitude, and the seatbelt sign came off. Passengers who needed the washroom were making their way to the back and front of the plane. Other passengers were getting stowed books to read and laptops to work on.

James acknowledged, "It has taken me fourteen years so far, and now I feel that I may be closing in on his last known whereabouts, for you see," he said as he pointed to a map. He had been making marks on it from the papers that he kept on his lap after removing them before Sam could sit on them earlier. "Hezron ended up working as a slave serving his new master, a camel caravan merchant who traveled to and from the Orient through the East India passage. In fact, most of the trade with the Orient was in the hands of Arabs, Himyarites, and Persians. He remained in captivity for approximately four years when his master brought him back from the Orient to a place he knew not. Are you sure I am not putting you to sleep as I do with my students? I find so few people genuinely interested."

Sam was trying to absorb it all. "I am fascinated, is it all right if I make a few notes as we go along?" he said as he retrieved his notepad from the inner sanctum of his jacket.

"My! You are interested? Can I ask you what parts fascinate you?" Professor James inquired.

"Oh, I read a lot of history books, biographies, and such, and if I ever can help one of my clients with their project, I would like to. So I will be keeping a look out for any relevant material that you might like. Is that alright with you? I would like to be able to contact you if I run across something?"

"Absolutely, I have people around the world doing just that, but usually they are in the same field as me. But I do have the odd one or two people who do things like this for a hobby and really do like volunteering for archeological digs during their holidays," James acknowledged

"So what happened to Hezron?" Sam said, working on bringing the Professor back in focus.

"Well, there he was ransomed by a Jewish merchant after the merchant learned that this slave, Hezron was a Jew. One document says it took thirty-two pieces of gold in the province of Azanian to purchase that freedom. And the reason given for the Jewish merchant to set Hezron free was that it was the year of Jubilee. If you are not familiar with the Year of Jubilee, every fifty years when Jews are required by God to set slaves free. The Jews no longer apply that rule today because they have lost track of which year is the Jubilee," James said as he turned and thanked the flight attendant for the food tray offered. Sam did the same.

"Please continue," Sam said, encouraging as he took a bite of his food. "So what happened to Hezron?"

"From there, I believe Hezron traveled to a dwelling place on an island south of Egypt and joined up with the tribe of Asher near Khanaqin. This land was ten miles across in all directions and encircled by waters. From the first moment before Shabbat began, fires were lit surrounding the river, and during that time, no human being could approach within half a mile of either side of it because of the fires. I believe it was during one of those Shabbat rests when Hezron brought forth the parchment he had been carrying with him for so long and revealed it. That is why it is the same Hezron documented as the one I am following and where I get some of what I know. I think there is more at the site." James paused to take a bite of the sandwich.

"So this is the reason for the trip to Egypt? What do you think you will find and where?" Sam said as he continued to encourage James to spill the beans.

James, happy to oblige, swallowed his food and continued, "Yes, but first I am going to stop off at Cairo to visit a friend before going to the dig where I believe Hezron visited. I have a friend out overseeing this archeological dig right now, and I believe it might even be the same village where Hezron grew up."

"Wow, interesting; I can see how you love your line of investigative work. Who is this friend in Cairo, and do you think he has some information to further your research project?" Sam remarked.

James nodded as he took another bite and, after washing it down with a drink, continued with, "My friend in Cairo has more cultural and biblical understandings of this area, and I enjoy visiting him when I get out this way. We go a long way back. Some important prophecies were in the parchment, and I believe Hezron wanted his tribal priests to look at it. My friend might be able to give me more insight into this. Smith recognized the parchment from the order of the Tzedek [also known as Melchizedek] from the city of Salem. Smith is said to have associated with Hezron regularly and even wrote a letter to the King of Egypt citing Hezron as wise and with extensive knowledge. It was Simah's letter requesting acceptance by his contemporaries as true, and with unquestionable authority did he ask the King to grant him freedom of travel and protection. That was one of the most interesting finds I have so far." James consumed the rest of his plate with gusto as he was engulfed in the story.

"So you must have made quite a few trips out this way over the years?" quizzed Sam.

"Actually, I was here recently for a seminar; come to think about it, it was a few years back. The speaker at the seminar was Dr. Goldberg, a friend of mine and whom I am now planning on visiting. He has been a friend since my college days, and he is now a professor and lecturer in the same field as me. I have found that his work and mine, while not the same, share a common era and group of people. I will be making sure that I get to his work site this trip," James said as he turned to let a passing flight attendant and asked for a blanket as they had the air conditioner up a might too much for his old body.

"Ohh, so what is the digging, and where is he now?" Sam said as he played with his cell phone in a pre-occupied way. Reminding himself to get Karen to dig up what information she could on Professor Goldberg, an archeologist.

"He has found an ancient town in Sudan, and my question is if an Alexandrian librarian came through as indicated by other documents I have read, or was it just the area where he was raised and may be returned to." James' thoughts drifted off as the smiling flight attendant asked if he needed anything else when she returned with the blanket. Giving the flight attendant a "Thank you" and smile when she laid it across her legs.

Turning back to the subject at hand, James asked. "What was I talking about... oh yes, Sudan, a beautiful country this time of the year." James' mind wandered in and out of several thoughts as he was about to speak.

"Your friend?" Sam said as he tried to help James stay on track.

"My friend?" Confused for a moment, James couldn't make any connections to what he was last talking about.

"Yes, the one you are going to visit while in Egypt," Sam said encouragingly.

"Oh, yes, he is digging at an ancient town, where he recently unearthed a stone tablet which is turning into a rather nice find. From what I understand, it is a Zodiac chart on stone." Now, remembering his thoughts, James continued, "Since that would be about the constellation, for which Hezron was famous, I believe he might have come across a village.

Hezron, whom I have been researching, may have been after he obtained the scroll."

Working the conversation around to his life work, Sam could see that Professor James Holden was a wealth of information regarding his studies. Still, Sam didn't see anything worthy of an investigator traveling the world following him, though. Sam noticed that the Professor was more than a little absent-minded and, given his age, attributed it to the first signs of Alzheimer's. For the most part, Professor Holden had only moments when he could not remember, probably the reason for so many sticky notes all over his books, messages, and files.

Crackling and a hissing sound within the lower body of the plane caused everyone to go silent. The plane shivered. The lights overhead flickered. Everyone in the cabin froze, waiting. A small child whimpered under the increased tension in the air among the adults around him. The pilot came on over the speakers to announce through static "**crackle*"…with the solar storm, there was some electrical field interference with the plane's communications system, but everything was alright. Please buckle up."

Sam and James look at each other as seasoned travelers do, but they soon were back to their conversation with an ear for any more announcements from the captain. "As I was saying," James said, picking up his conversation where he left off. "Studying this Ethiopian, who claimed to be Jewish, once a librarian at the Alexandria library, slave to traveling merchants, almost killed on several occasions, is hard to track down and has been my latest research project for over fourteen years. He is a fascination or, some say, an obsession of mine." James chuckled more to himself like it was a private joke.

"So, what have you learned so far that keeps you wanting more out of this particular research project?" Sam inquired.

"I think the connection of the scroll makes to the constellations and their importance, in almost every document I have read on Hezron, has me most fascinated. While bits and pieces have been revealed in parchments and other historical records, only one theme remains. Hezron became wise in understanding the prophecies and their relationship to the constellations. He was renowned in any comments made mention by those who knew him or of him and the scroll," James explained, stretching in his seat, trying to get comfortable after sitting for so long.

Sam could not see how this held the kind of importance or why the curator was paying him to follow him around the world. As far as Sam could tell, Professor James was researching some historically dusty trail of a man of the fourth century. He tried to look interested, attentively asking questions hoping that something would stand out and give him something to report back to the curator. "So, the connection between the scrolls and what is written in them is ultimately your fascination?" Sam ventured to guess.

"Yes, my son, bless his heart, is taking classes at a Jewish University called Yeshiva University in New York. They have a Rabbi theological seminary where rabbinate training helps us understand better, as John, my son," James proudly announced before continuing, "is taking classes and focusing on things our research has brought forth so far. A great place to do some of the background sides of the research, not that he is working towards any rabbinate doctorate, mind you."

"So, what has he uncovered for you?" Sam asked now that he had got the Professor enthusiastically talking about his favorite subject.

James mulled the question over in his mind before answering, "I think it was the connection of the twelve tribes to the constellation."

"How so?" Sam said, now puzzled.

James smiled and said, "Somewhere in scripture, in Genesis, I don't exactly where, it says that the lights of heaven, stars and such, God said they are to be for signs."

"Ok, so how does this have anything to do with the tribes of Israel?" Sam pushed for more insight.

"According to my son John, who is researching the religious aspects of this project, pointed out an interesting connection. Scripture says, 'Jesus said that in the end time there will be a sign in the sky, of the son of man in heaven,' whatever that means. John tied it to the Virgo sign for his first coming and birth. He also pointed out at the end with the Leo sign, as the Lion of the tribe of Judah."

"Yes, but what has that to do with the tribes of Israel?" Sam persisted.

"From what my son has gathered, Adam was given the right to name all the animals of the earth. God named the stars himself. He checked into this further and found those names for the constellations of the same variant in all ancient nations. So, it is no coincidence that the figures pictured in the Zodiac are the same, even if they do not carry the same meaning. So the logical question is, what signs and connections did the Hebrews make. " James said, pausing to gather his thoughts, "according to my son, Moses attributed the twelve signs to the twelve tribes. He thought it might have something to do with Joseph's dream. He said that Moses lined the houses of each tribe by zodiac order while on the pilgrimage in the wilderness. So many sprinklings of this thought are even mentioned in Josephus's writings. Josephus, one of my favorite historians, was the most accurate and articulate Jewish historian of his generation. John found Josephus stating they were named by Seth."

Sam interrupted, "So which do you think is right?"

"Who knows? All I can gather is the scroll Hezron had was very ancient. You have to understand that by Hezron's time in the fourth century, the connection between faith and constellations was not commonly practiced or taught. Not saying there is no evidence of a connection. In fact, Beth Alpha's floor is renowned as one of the most important mosaics in Israel. This synagogue is now part of the National Park on Kibbutz Hafzibah. It has a constellation of the floor of the Beth Alpha synagogue. If you are ever in Jerusalem, you should go see it," James encouraged.

Obviously, the Professor was caught up in the exuberance of his research. The one good thing Sam came out of this conversation with was Professor James' might use his company 'if conditions warranted it. At least he had that much to report for progress to the curator.

When they arrived in Cairo, Sam made a call to Mr. Bloomberg. Sam said, while he juggled with his notebook. "Professor James believes that the scroll that Hezron had in his possession was an ancient scroll on the prophecy and its connection to the constellations."

Mr. Bloomberg jumped all over that with, "Then we want an extraction team close by. Keep me posted."

Sam had jotted down what he thought were the highlights of his conversation, "… and I was able to offer our 'extraction team' services should Professor James require it. He thinks I am part of an international border brokerage firm with capabilities that might be of interest to him," Sam said, then paused, "as an undercover story, you understand." That seemed to impress the curator at the other end of the line.

"Nice tie-in, Sam. That is great." Mr. Bloomberg verbally patted Sam on the back.

Sam thought this was an excellent opportunity to get the curator to explain why this particular parchment is so essential. "So, what is on this parchment that is so important to you?"

Mr. Bloomberg just pushed him to "keep following and report back." he said, brushing off any further questions and reminding him, "You know as much as you need to know." At least, that is what Sam thought he heard through the crackling of the phone line.

"All right, I will continue to report, but if the Professor finds any parchments, I am not going to physically take it away from him. I believe that the supposed age of parchment, and the probable fragility if found, would warrant your extraction teams' delicate handling. Secondly, there is no need for me to take parchments that turn out to be of no interest to anyone but the Professor. I am not capable of determining that, nor sure I could handle something that fragile. I believe the Professor is more than capable of handling any artifact like the one he was describing."

"We can work with that. No doubt in good hands with the Professor as to its care. It is the knowledge contained within I want to be secured from his study," Sam heard the curator say grudgingly.

Obviously, the curator wouldn't budge on divulging why the value of the 'knowledge contained within' was so important, so Sam hung up the phone rather abruptly, dissatisfied, and after a looking around at his surroundings, he smiled. He thought it might be nice to have a vacation on someone else's dollar. The thought of spending someone else's money cheered him up as he gathered his luggage and weaved his way through the crowd, following after the Professor down the corridor.

Cairo's International Airport is one of the fastest growing airports in the Middle East, which means that a lot of the new buildings have a more comprehensive range of traveler amenities and new terminals, which Sam was now walking through. Sam waved at the Professor and pretended that now that they had arrived at the airport, they would be parting company and going their separate ways.

Upon procuring a car, Sam, without delay, followed the Professor's hotel shuttle van down a new airport access road that links the airport with the Cairo Ring Road. Sam remembered the last time he tried to get out of the airport and the congestion. He liked this improvement. While in the car, he called Karen, and when she answered the phone, he interrupted her greeting with, "Hey, it's me, safely in Cairo, presently following the Professor. I need you to do some research on Professor Goldberg for me. It sounds like from the conversation I had with Holden, he will be visiting his site this trip." Before there was much more conversation, the line went dead. The signal was gone.

Musing in his mind on the flight with the Professor, Sam mulled over the idea of befriending the man. Maybe I could hook up with him later and again offer his company's assistance, thus killing two birds with one stone. But shaking his head at his thoughts, he decided it just was not logical given his cover story to the Professor. How would he explain the paths crossing again if the scholar does not call him for assistance?

It was not long before they arrived at the hotel; Sam watched James book his accommodations from a discreet distance within the vast and elegant lobby. He left to find his own suitable accommodations nearby, figuring James would take some time to shower the travel dust off. While Sam was gone, James dropped off his bags in his room and left to see a friend in Cairo. James had called the local car rental place and had them bring a car around to the hotel for him. They were swift and had the car provided for him by the time he entered the lobby.

Sam never saw James leave in the car as he was occupied getting his own dust off with a nice shower in his hotel room across the street. He was delighted to procure a suite directly across the road, where he could watch the comings and goings of the Professor. Wrapped up in a towel, he checked out his window across the street to see if he could see any movement from Holden's room, and it looked strangely dark.

Chapter 6

Karen headed to the Professor's home to check in on it and see if there were any other clues as to what was so important, why the curator wanted a private investigator to follow him, and if there was anything that would help the investigation. Her car quit, leaving her to watch in apprehension and fascination as the sky tingled in a gray haze. For a brief second, she thought she saw the skeletal outline of her hands on the steering wheel. Other vehicles on the road experienced the same shutdown, and quite a few of the drivers got out of the car to look around. It didn't last all that long, and everything soon returned to normal. She turned on her radio to catch any reports and what was the probable cause.

When the show was over, and traffic started to move again, her car started, and she continued to the warehouse a little disconcerted. Arriving at the place, she noticed two young fellows enter the home, and shortly after that, one left. That was curious since her intel did not report any young fellows living at his place. She decided to keep a closer eye on this and do a little more digging.

She called Sam while sitting in the car, explaining to him about the new development. "Hey Sam, I just spotted two young college-age students at the Professor's place." Her cell phone cut out in the middle of the transmission and died, and she wondered if her phone was the only one affected this way.

She tried different things, including hitting the phone to get it to function, and after a while, it returned to a working state, and she was able to get a hold of Sam and finish their conversation. "Sam, it was weird, there was an eerie bluish green color to the air, and we all lost our color and went gray. I thought for a moment that I could see right through my skin and look at my skeleton as I lifted my hands up before me, but it was over before I got a chance to figure out what happened."

Sam commented, "That really does sound weird. Hope there is nothing to that. We have been having a lot of strange things going on lately. There is a lot of static on the phone at my end. Do you think the solar flares have something to do with this? By the way, how does your end sound?" he said, checking the phone for bars.

Karen listens hard as Sam's voice drifts in and out, "The phones have been acting really weird lately, working sometimes and other times not. Since we have the best the money can buy and have had no problems up to now, I do not understand why we keep losing our connection. Now back to the reason I called," he said, and at that point, the call was dropped, with Karen walking around trying to get a signal and speaking into the phone, "Can you hear me now?" he said only to realize that she had already lost connection. Pushing the redial, she is soon reconnected with Sam and, without preamble, said, "Before I lose you again. Two young fellows are at the Professor's place. Do you have any idea who they might be? As far as I have gathered, the Professor lives alone."

Sam replied with a plausible explanation, "Curator mentioned something about a son who is helping him on his project, so it might be him and one of his friends," he said, blocking one ear to hear her out of the other.

"Should I follow these fellows, or should I wait until they leave and get pictures?" Karen asked, trying to make out what Sam was saying.

Sam tossed both suggestions around in his mind with a tilting of his head to the left and right as he pondered for a moment before saying, "I think we need pictures more. I wish there was a way of following up on both. Find out what you can on the son, though. Let me know what you do find out."

It wasn't too long after that the other fellow returned, and the two left together. She could only presuppose they were going out for something to eat as her stomach growled at her. She waited until they were well out of sight before attempting to enter the warehouse.

It was an old lock and easy to pick. Karen entered the house quickly, scanning it for anything of interest. She noticed the papers on the table. Examining a couple of pages, got enough info to call the curator to ask him if this was of any interest. The curator said yes, that was good information, and could she make a copy of it. She took out her camera and started getting pictures of each page. There were so many pages, and she started getting nervous that she had been here too long.

It was getting dark outside, making it harder and harder to catch some natural light in the room, and she was not going to turn on the lights because the last thing she needed was to draw suspicion about her activities. As it was, it went smoothly, and soon she was out the door and heading back to her car.

The local gang had noticed the woman going into the house and then left and figured that whatever she took must be valuable. They sneaked up as she was putting the key in her car door and grabbed her from behind. Dragging the struggling woman further into the alley was more challenging, but one solid punch to the chin helped. Up against the car, they searched her for the goods. This woman came to, in a flurry of moves, was giving them all quite a struggle, more than they expected. They were finally able to overwhelm her and hold her down while one of them finished searching her. There wasn't much, a couple dollars in her pocket, the lock pick, which he kept, and the camera. While one of them was looking at the camera, the boys lost their hold on her, and she bolted. He called the boys off, saying that she wasn't worth it.

It wasn't, but two seconds later, they heard the car squeal, and the subsequent silence was short-lived. Figuring that it was time to move on, the gang members turned just as police cars appeared from all directions. They were cornered. Everyone split, but nobody even made it out of the alley. The officers quickly arrested them on a murder charge and took everything away as evidence. They figured their arrested leader must have ratted them out for a lighter sentence.

Unbeknownst to Karen, her lock pick and camera were heading to the police station. All she knew was that she could not report the camera stolen because the lockpick would incriminate her. She had a dilemma on her hands.

She called Sam as she drove away, "Hey, Sam, you would not believe what just happened?"

"What?"

"Four guys just ganged up on me right after I left the Professor's place and robbed me. They besieged me and got a lucky punch in. I did have the element of surprise when they thought they finally had me under control, and I was able to escape. However, without my camera or pick," she said, still breathing a little short from the struggle, tenderly touching the chin and checking to see tears in her shirt and dirt on her face when she looked in the mirror.

Sam asked, "Are you alright?"

Karen smiled at her partner's concern. "Yeah, I now realize this cushy job has made me out of shape for fieldwork, and I should have been better able to handle the situation. So here I am with just a few scrapes and bruises, mostly in my pride."

And once re-assured she merely suffered minor bruises and scrapes, he nodded his head at the dilemma. "Glad to hear that. Will, you be reporting this to the police?"

Mulling the issue at hand, Karen said, "And what explanation am I going to give the police about the pick and camera? And why was I in that part of town? And what would happen if the officers wanted to get more info? Like the who, what, where, and why I was there in the first place? I don't have answers for that. Let me turn up the police scanner; I think something happened in the same alley I was attacked in. "She had turned on the police radio scanner, and together they listened to the ensuing capture of the murderer and the location.

Karen got back on the phone. "I was robbed in that alley no more than two minutes ago, and they must have arrived immediately after I left. That could easily mean that the police now have my camera, and I believe they have just arrested the same ones who attacked me on another charge."

Sam asked, "Are you interested in getting another camera and lock pick and taking some more photos of the material you found?" he said.

She rubbed her forehead like a headache was coming on full blast, closing her eyes, and leaning her head back against the seat rest. "Sam, let me think about that one. I have had enough for one night, and I am going home for a good soak and relax. In fact, now that I think about it, I will call it a night. I will call you in the morning when I have made my decision. Right now, just say goodnight, Sam," she said and clicked the cell phone closed.

Besides, she thought, the injuries were screaming at her as she rolled her neck and shoulders, trying to work out the kinks. The articles stolen weren't going anywhere anytime soon as far as she could see. Maybe she could go back to the alley tomorrow and find the pieces dropped during the scuffle.

It was a farfetched hope at best. *But you never know*, she thought.

"Ugh, I am giving this too much thought," she said to herself. She knew in her heart it was a fat chance, but even a slim one she was willing to check out. It was a small ray of hope as she continued to go over what had transpired. She was sure they would not rat on her because it would incriminate them. "At least that was one less thing to think about," she said aloud, glad no one was around to hear her.

Arriving home, a beautiful little cottage down a narrow lane out in the peaceful country was a welcome sight. In the door, Karen quickly shed her torn clothes and threw them in the fireplace. She set it ablaze, turned on the bath water, and mixed herself a nice hot toddy to soothe her nerves. These last few years behind the desk had taken their toll on her ability to defend herself, which really infuriated her. She should have been able to beat the living crap out of all of them.

While waiting for the clothes to burn up and the water to fill the tub, she decided to see what caused the police to pick up that group so quickly. Her vast connections within the Bureau left her with resources that came in handy. It turns out they were the garden variety thugs hanging around looking for trouble and getting plenty of petty thief crimes and raps sheets. Nothing had yet been posted on the latest arrests. With that, she turned off her computer and slowly headed into the bathroom to have that long-awaited soak that her body so badly needed. She was starting to stove up, and a long soak in her favorite therapeutic fragrant bath oil would be just what the doctor ordered.

Chapter 7

Hearing a critical turn in the lock, Travis scrambled to think of what he was going to say. Whoever it was, had more rights to be here than he did since they had the key to the place and they were with the police. He decided the best approach was the honest one. The door started to open, so boning up on his courage, Travis jumped up swiftly, headed to the door, took the beam off, and opened it the rest of the way with a flourish, bowed low like a butler welcoming the master back to his home. John, the Professor's son, was so startled that he dropped his keys as the police officers with guns drawn flanked John in a protective stance before advancing further into the building.

John was shocked to find someone in his father's house, especially since his dad had not mentioned leaving anyone there to look after the place. John quickly recovered, firing off a string of questions. "Who are you? How did you get in here? And what are you doing here? He said and, looking closer, declared as a thought crossed his mind, "And why are you still here?"

Travis interrupted with, "Hi, my name is Travis O'Reilly, and I know this looks really suspicious, but I witnessed a murder and was seen. They came after me, and I ended up in the dead end of an alley behind this place. I admit breaking into this place to escape."

"Sir, could you put your hands behind your back and face the wall?" the officer said. With compliance, the officer soon had Travis handcuffed and sitting on the sofa for questioning.

John watched and observed all the interaction between the police officer and the man in his father's place, now handcuffed and sitting on the sofa, looking confident. John nodded to himself, thinking Travis did not look or seem like the typical burglar, and he sure didn't behave like one either. Travis continued, "Could I ask to speak to a homicide detective in charge of a recent murder in the next alley over?" he said to the police officer who had been questioning him.

More officers moved into the room, and John walked around checking to see how much was disturbed or taken. Police officers were taking down information, from Travis, on the man outside the window, his presence in the room, and the murder he had witnessed. After John got off the phone after calling his father to report what had occurred, he sat beside Travis on the sofa in the living room so that he could find out more, "Exactly why did you remain in my dad's place long after the crime had been committed?"

"Those thugs never left the area, and there was always one at the entrance to the alley." Travis pointed up to the window where he had been watching. When Travis mentioned the thugs that hung out at the corner, John had a perfect idea of which ones. Travis went on to say, "These are the ones who killed the man in the alley." Then it all started to make sense.

While waiting for the homicide detective to arrive, John and Travis moved on to other subjects, like what they did for a living and the exciting research the Professor he was currently investigating was doing. They were soon oblivious to the milling around of the officers as they did their job.

The fact that Travis had been reading about it while waiting became evident when he explained. "I have to admit reading the notes on Hezron that were on the Professor's desk and the notes on the refrigerator. I must apologize for making myself at home," he said, taking this opportunity to ask a police officer if it was alright for him to sweep up the glass on the floor." But from what I read about the parchment that Hezron is supposed to have possessed, I was hooked. I was incredibly excited about the connection to the planetary details. That is my field of study."

"What do you mean your field?" John asked.

"You see, I am an Astronomy student, and my major thesis is on near objects. Actually, I am an astrophysicist student working on my doctorate. One of the most fascinating studies is on Planet X. It has been photographed by the Russians recently, and NASA saw it too. It is a dark object, almost like a black hole, currently hiding behind the sun. You know that the sun has not had sun spots since its arrival?" Travis explained.

"Sorry, I am not making the connection," John said, shaking his head.

"OK, let me back up for a second here. Come with me," Travis said as he moved with permission from the police officer at the desk and pointed to one document. "From what I understand, this parchment your father is looking for may be documentation of the sighting of the last visit of Planet X," he said. When moving over to the kitchen, he saw his note, reminding him to clear his account; he grabbed the money and note and handed it to John as the officers watched Travis and John. "I paid for all I ate too. Sorry, I was hungry," he said, shrugging it off, pointing to the other notes on the refrigerator. "He wrote on one of the scratch pads stickies on the refrigerator the name, Niribu, which Plant X was known by back then. They, and by that, I mean some of my fellow astrophysicists, say that it triggers earthquakes, unleashes tsunamis around the world as it passes by, and even opens up volcanoes. There is some theory that it may have caused the last ice age by turning this world on its axis," Travis explained.

"Turned on its axis?!" John exclaimed. "I didn't know that happened," he said, eyes widening as the thoughts of what Travis said sunk in.

"It is just one theory." Travis shrugged as he continued to expand. "It has been declared as the one who destroyed Maldek, the missing planet which is now our asteroid belt that you find between Earth and Mars. They say that it causes the big craters and surface scars on the moon and other planets of our solar system as well as the reason for their varying axial tilts and orbits."

John stopped Travis there. "Isn't that a bit much for just one space object to do?"

Travis shook his head. "Nope, this is one mother lode. It could even stop our planet from orbiting or take our world entirely out of orbit when it is within range."

"What!!" John declared. "You can not be serious."

Travis nodded, "Right now, it seems as if the sun and this planet are holding each other hostage, but if it suddenly ricochets out of the sun's magnetic field, it will slingshot, and the worry is that it will be in our direction."

John interrupted Travis again, "So how is what you are describing related to my dad's work?"

Travis said, "One," holding up his index finger, "the names are the same." "Two," holding up two fingers, "the effects Planet X is having on other objects it has passed by so far this time are the same effects documented. Your father has it on his desk. And three, both are known to have wings," he said holding up a third finger. "That is why I think Planet X and Niribu are one and the same," he said with finality.

"Wait a minute, you might be on to something here," John said, snapping his fingers, jumped up, and went to the library shelf and removed a book that he brought back to the table. He opened it up to the page where a photo of a clay tablet was displayed. "There was this clay tablet uncovered in the Near East many years ago. On the tablet, the Sumerians jotted down something that looked like our solar system. Everything is here, except not quite in their places. Earth was there, and Saturn and Jupiter, as well as all the other planets we know today. Ohhhhh, and one other thing, the clay tablet clearly displays eleven planets. What was really weird, the eleventh planet was called the 'Winged One.'"

"Travis O'Reilly," he said, jarring their train of thought and interrupting their conversation, the officer in charge said. Two police officers from the homicide division walked up. One introduced himself. "Lieutenant Millar and this is Lieutenant Spencer," he said, getting down to business. "You have requested to speak to us regarding a murder you witnessed. Could you please state and spell your name. Could you tell us what you witnessed?"

By this time, John has convinced Travis not only innocent but is genuinely caught up in witnessing a crime. John is confident that, with his knowledge of the galaxies, Travis just might be able to help his father and himself in their quest. He turned to the officer in charge and asked that Travis not be charged with any break and entering, given the extenuating circumstances. John informed the officers when they asked again and would not be pressing charges for break and entry and trespassing, as Travis's use of the home as a hideout from the hoodlums was excusable in this case. John wanted to make sure no charges were laid against Travis for trespassing, so he called his father and, once he had him on the line, handed the phone over to the officer so that his father could verify that he would not lay charges. The police officer reassured John, "Travis as a witness to a murder is far more important."

Under the protection of the police, Travis went out to the murder site, pointed out, described what he saw, what happened, and how he subsequently arrived and felt forced to stay at the Professor's home until now. One of the detectives requested Travis to come down to the police department and give a written statement. John took Travis in his car, following the patrol vehicle to the police station, as Travis would also need transportation back. Besides, they were just getting started on finding out what each other knew.

It was early afternoon when Travis and John finally left the police station. John had extended the invitation for Travis to stay for the night at his apartment suite on campus. Travis gladly accepted, but John remembered that he needed to pick up the papers, which was the original reason for going to his father's place. When they got there, both of their stomachs were grumbling. John mentioned, "I don't have much in the way of food at the apartment."

Travis said, "There is here," heading to the kitchen. So together, they kidded around in the kitchen as they found stuff to make a good chili dinner. With Travis's culinary skills at the fixings and cooking, John gathered up the papers he thought his father had asked for.

John called his father, guessing that he should have arrived in Egypt by now, and it would be a good time to bring him up to speed as to what had transpired and give him the information requested. He was looking forward to it. He had some news of his own that he was very excited to share. "Hi, Dad. So have you arrived safe and sound in Cairo?" he asked. After listening to his father's response, he declared, "Boy, do I have a lot of things to tell you. Your place has been broken into by a nice guy who used the place as a hideout. He was the one witnessing a murder in the neighborhood, and you should meet him. That is why I had you tell the police that you will not be pressing breaking and entry charges. I hope that is OK with you?" he said as he continued, and his voice picked up a more excited tone. "Travis, that is the guy I found staying at your place; he has made a connection between Niribu and the 'winged one.' Anyway, he is interested in Hezron and what he knew about Niribu," he said, throwing all these thoughts at his father at once. "He is making connections between the constellations and what was on the clay tablet I think you will find very interesting. Anyway, I have got to go; I will call you right back. "Bye," he said when he spotted Travis bringing out the hot chili. He did not give his father much of a chance to talk. He would apologize later. The chili just smelt so good.

John and Travis settled down in the living room, and since there was a lull in the conversation, with only the sounds of spoons digging and chewing, John decided this would be an excellent time to bring Travis up to speed on his contribution to the research project. Travis had become highly interested since making the connection between his studies and Hezron's Niribu. John decided a little inside information with the background on Hezron might help Travis. "I am going to give you some background information, at least the religious aspects I have been studying. By the way, this chili is awesome."

"Thank you," Travis said, taking a slight head bow of acknowledgment. "Sure, backgrounds are always good."

"Alright, "John says, thinking about the most recent addition to his storehouse of knowledge. "My focus and contribution is the background on the religion of this time period, which we estimate could be when the parchment was written. Anyway, I had an interesting meeting one night with a rabbi in the library a few months ago. He had noticed me because of the books I was taking out and, after looking over my shoulder, must have confirmed in his mind that I might like to learn more about the Tzadik."

Tavis, looking confused, asked, "Tzadik?"

John conspiratorially leans forward and, with a smile creeping across his face, says, "Have you ever heard of Melchizedek?"

Travis shook his head. "No"

John leans back. "I will give you a hint. Hebrew 7:11 "If therefore perfection were by the Levitical priesthood, what further need was there that another priest should rise after the order of Melchizedek, and not be called after the order of Aaron."

As it dawns on him, Travis utters, "Jesus," feeling good that he knew something from his Sunday school classes.

John nodded his head. "I am not going to ask you to believe this story I am about to tell you."

Travis leaning forward, said, "OK."

John excitedly blurted, "The family of David is a special line of priests."

Travis scowled." Are you talking about King David in the Bible?"

John nods. "Yep, and I can prove it to you, although it is only hinted at. Now, where is that Bible," he said, getting up. He pulled it off the shelf, quickly flipped it to 2 Samuel 8:18, and pointed it out to Travis. "David's sons were chief ministers. I bet you are thinking, no big deal.. Right? OK, in Hebrew, it reads, "uVenayahu Ben Yohoyada vehakreti venality uvenei David cohanim hayu."

Travis, lost on all those Hebrew words, at least caught one piece, "David cohamin?"

John nodded. "David is a Cohen, which is a special line of the Levi priests." Laying the Bible down, John elaborated, "The only possible translation for the word Cohen in the Bible is priest, so how could the sons of David be priests?"

Travis was guessing, "One of David's wives was from the family of priests?"

John, shaking his head, said, "Kahuna, which means priesthood is only transmitted by males." Picking up the Bible again, John went to 2 Samuel 20:26 and, speaking Hebrew read, "vegan Ira haywire haya cohen l'David" which John translated as "Also Ira, the Jairite was a priest unto David,"... laying the book down again John asked, "So who are the Jairites?

Travis was feeling a bit out of his league and, wondering where this was all going, shook his head. "You got me," he said, taking another mouthful of chili in.

John seeing that he has just about completely lost, Travis explained, "Now, I hate to seem to be giving you a Bible study, but it is the background I have been studying for my father, and I want you to see this. So if it is OK with you, let me show you some more."

Travis, willing to see where this all was going, gives his consent. "OK, I give, go on."

But the rest of John's thoughts were interrupted by the authoritative knock on the door, and the "NYPD" announcement followed. John went to the door and asked, "Who is it?" through the closed door.

The men on the other side of the door responded with, "Detective Millar and Spencer, Homicide Division." John let them in, and they beeline directly towards Travis. "We have just made an arrest and wanted you to come with us to identify the murderer."

John stepped up and offered, "That was fast. I will bring Travis and follow in my own car."

Detective Millar said, "Here will be the procedures we will follow. Upon arriving at the police station, I will bring you to my desk and have you look through some photos of those that fit your description.

You may see the suspect in amongst the photos. Please identify the man you saw makes the killing in the alley. Next, we will take you to a room where you will look through the two-way window and see if any of the men we have gathered are involved in the murder and subsequent chase. We wanted you to identify any of the perpetrators. Do you understand the procedure?"

"Why do I have to identify them in photos if you have suspects already at the station?' Travis asked.

"Mistaken identity plays seventy-five percent of cases overturned. If mistaken eyewitness identification plays a role in all those discovered cases, imagine how many are wrongfully charged and even convicted. Our policy is when identifying a suspect, the eyewitness, that is, you will be shown a group of six photos at once. Then we will show you a lineup of six men, which you can see if you can identify the one who committed the murder. Then we will look at six photos one at a time, and you again get to identify the culprit. We do not often get to reevaluate the accuracy of the eyewitness. Your testimony is valuable, and with verification of the certainty of your eyewitness capabilities, we may be able to secure a solid case against the perpetrator in this case."

The detectives were on top of this and anxious to create a strong rationale because everything fit the profile of several others cases in the area. They had someone who witnessed the latest murder allowing them to lay some serious charges on the gang. They had been suspicious of the leader of other violent crimes in the area for quite some time. You could almost see the detectives salivate over this breakthrough.

Following the police car down to the police station with Travis in the passenger seat of John's car, John turned left. "So you find our research project interesting?"

Travis laughed. "Yes, it has always been a side interest of mine, and how the ancients viewed the constellations has been a sideline study when I get an opportunity."

"Well then, how about if I ask my father if you can come on our latest research trip with me during our spring break?" John offered. "I think you will be a valuable asset to the research team. And if not, we can continue to compare notes while you are in town."

"Sure," Travis said, accepting the invitation. "That works for me as I have officially started my spring break and do not have anything to rush back for."

"Cool, me too," John responded as they pulled up to the police station. John stayed behind in the car to call for glass replacement for the window and lock changes for the building. He was able to have it arranged that both would be there at the same time later that day.

Once Travis correctly identified the murderer in the lineup. And again, in the photos and all the information the police needed. It was mid-morning by the time it was all over. Travis left the police station and found John still waiting in the car. They headed back out towards the Professor's home, stopping at the hotel first so that Travis could collect his stuff. They needed to get over to the Professor's house and wait for the repairmen to show up. John stopped at Travis's hotel. Travis ran up to the front desk to settle his account. He was informed that his baggage was now sitting in the manager's office. He paid his tab, collected his luggage, and was back out the door before John would have to move the car.

While waiting in the car, John called his father and, upon getting through, jumped in with, "Dad, sorry for the delay and hanging up on you earlier, before you even had a chance to talk. Now, what do you need? I have picked up the files on the right side of your desk, but I was so asleep when you called, I am not sure if I remember all of what you were asking me to pick up." he said, grabbing a pen and paper.

"I forgot," James mumbled, struggling to remember why he called in the first place. "Why don't you join me and bring it all with you? That way, I will have them? You know the files we went over together last week, and that should do it."

"Hey, Dad, Travis, the guy I met at your place knows about Niribu. He is not doing anything at the moment. He is an astrophysicist student and can make sense of the historical documents we are working on.

He is so into what we are researching I believe he would be a valuable asset to our work," he said, checking the interest on Travis's face as he got into the car.

Travis nodded.

"Why don't I see if he wants to come with me, and then you can meet him? I believe he would be a beneficial advantage on our team."

Travis knew he would be free for a couple of months before the university classes began again, so this would be great. His eyes lit up. He was already fascinated with the project and the material he had read so far, and if he could help the Professor put the pieces to the puzzle together, that would be an extra bonus. So while John was on the phone waiting for his father's answer, he was prepared to give, with his resounding 'yes, 'a victory fist in the air.

After saying, "Good, see you in Jerusalem then, bye for now, and be safe," John closed the cell phone and grinned at Travis. John gave him the thumbs up. "I say we have a yes, all expenses trip winner here," he said, as Travis exuberantly yelled, "Yes," and almost put his fist through the roof of the car. John laughed. All settled. Travis was going on an all-expense trip to the Middle East with John to help with Professor Holden's archeological study.

As Travis entered the dorm room, he turned to John and asked, "You remember mentioning the winged one?"

John nodded.

"May I use your computer? You do have Internet, I hope?" he said, spotting John's computer surrounded and almost buried by the piles of study paper and books.

Again John nodded and pointed to his desk and laptop.

Travis swiftly grabbed a seat at the computer. "I want to show you something." With a few keystrokes, he quickly brought up Google Images and typed 'Niribu winged one.' Google loaded up pages under that description. On the first page, there were images of a red disc much like the moon during an eclipse when it turns blood red, except this one had vapor on either side of it shaped like hazed blue wings.

What John saw over Travis's shoulder impressed him. "Wow, I see what you are saying."

Travis rattled off what he knew off the top of his head. "Planet X is about 100 times the size of Earth with an elliptical orbit that takes it far out into the galaxy and back every 3600 years. This picture looks like they did document its proper visual position from Earth. Some think that it is not a real planet but what they call a brown dwarf, which is a massive ball of dust and gas that almost succeeded in becoming its own star. The interesting thing about this planet is that once it is here, it accelerates in speed and swings really close to the sun, disrupting everything it comes close to."

"So, how long has it been observed?" John asked, continuing to look over Travis's shoulder at the images.

"In the spring of 2003, it suddenly made its appearance, not by a sighting, but by the other celestial objects' reaction to its presence in the outer regions of our solar system. It was observed and finally photographed as it reached the inner regions of our solar system. Some disturbing behaviors of Jupiter were observed as it passed. We have been trying to project its path by the Earth, but everything is inconclusive while it and the sun are battling it out. We have yet to see it come from the other side of the sun where it is now, which has thrown off all our original calculations. Every once in a while, someone would claim to have seen it peek out on the other side of the sun, only to have it be pulled back. We do not see or hear much on the subject since it has been 'classified.' by the US government agency." Travis answered with a sigh.

Some papers slipped out of John's hands, and John, quick on the reflex, managed to catch them mid-flight. One of them catches John's eye. In John's father's handwriting was a sticky note with eclipses circled. John read the paper upon which the sticky note was attached, and a thought hit John. He tells Travis to "move," giving Travis a shove and immediately jumps into the chair facing his computer.

Travis took it upon himself to check out the sleeping accommodations and the facilities as he was beginning to smell, confirmed by the quick sniff under the armpit; he wrinkled his nose, yep, he stunk. John's vague, "Make yourself at home," wave away with the back of his hand, without even looking up from the computer screen, was all Travis needed. Travis found what he was looking for in the bathroom. Travis soon availed himself of what could be best described as an old toothbrush found at the bottom of his backpack, along with toothpaste and rinse. Before brushing his teeth, he pulled a few hairs caught between the bristles. Rinsing them under the hot water tap and turning on the shower. It was beginning to look like the tables were turning for the better, Travis thought as he inspected his teeth and face in the mirror. He grinned to himself as he hummed, divesting himself of his clothing and stepping into the shower.

Refreshed and comfortable in a pair of slippers and a lounging robe he had found hanging behind the bathroom door, he headed back to the kitchenette for another snack. Turning on the radio in the kitchen, Travis was able to pick up a news broadcast report, "Northern lights were seen at the equator, a rare occurrence." Travis gathered up his clothing and threw them into the washing machine as he listened to the broadcast. Travis nodded to himself. Solar flares have started. Upon settling down on the sofa behind John, he noticed some papers sticking out from under the books lying on the study desk. And it was the last he remembered as he drifted off to sleep.

It took little time before John was jumping through a myriad of websites. First, he pulled up NASA's eclipse charts that Travis had pulled up earlier, the Jewish calendar of feasts dates, and some other websites of historical events. Checking the dates to see if anything occurred on those dates. He was so caught up in his research he didn't even hear Travis sneak up behind him. Travis asked him, "So what have you found so interesting?" and scared the crap out of John. Travis stretched the kinks out from his nap.

Once he regained his heartbeat and calmed down, John explained his theory. "In the notes that I picked up, there was a question, 'is the blood red moon of prophecy the same as an eclipse?' That got me thinking about what you said and what one of my professors mentioned in one of my classes. The Professor brought up Sir Isaac Newton's hypothesis on Daniel 9:24, something about 'seven weeks' starting when Israel captures Jerusalem. That start date, according to him, should be for the 'going forth and building Jerusalem' June 7, 1967." Pointing to a website, he said, "with 'days are years' for prophetic calculations, I need to work out what day that lands on. See if any eclipses or feasts tied themselves together with either the historical events or each other."

Travis listened in disbelief. He has never known passion for this religious stuff, but then he never thought it had anything to do with the here and now either. This was getting more and more intertwined. Maybe this was why Hezron's scroll was having such an effect upon its hearers and readers. Not that Travis or John was able to come to any conclusions at the moment. So John printed out several websites and made a new file of his own on the zodiac, feasts, eclipses, and several historical websites that charted significant events, for countries and for the Jews, along with other things off of NASA's website. He thought that he might get a chance to study this idea during a quiet period while on the flight over and later be able to show his father the concept and see what he thought.

Travis went to check on his clothes in the dryer and found them ready to put back on. He disappeared into the bathroom for a moment and was soon back out dressed. It was good to get into clean clothes.

John invited Travis to come with him back to his father's place to meet with the repairmen, who should be arriving within the next hour or so. An unearthly gray glow appeared before his vision, and everywhere Travis looked, it was like he had x-ray vision. Travis saw John's skeleton walk, which was really weird. At that moment, he remembered, so this is what an x-ray sun flare does in the New York smog.

John was transfixed, looking around him, wondering what was going on, and looked at Travis only to see him in radiographic skeletal form.

Travis quickly explained, "This is an x-ray sun flare which will only last a short period. It comes without warning because it travels at the speed of light. When the sun sends one of these, it only takes eight minutes to get to Earth. Most of it is absorbed in the ionosphere when it hits our atmosphere. Because it is so highly charged, it creates such a reactive environment, so we see the air we breathe turn into x-ray film vision right before our eyes. Given New York's air pollution, we may be getting more visual effects than, let's say, someone out in the country," and laughed at the expression of wonderment on John's face as he marveled, looking at his skeletal frame and hands.

Travis explained further, "There is an aircraft halfway between the Earth and the sun with sensors onboard monitoring and measuring the energy and the intensity of the solar winds, flares, and storms. They figure this one will be big, but it is proving to be a massive one. One thing that they are concerned with, though, is how it will affect the magnetic configuration of Earth's geomagnetic field. If it hits at a time when both the sun's and the Earth's magnetic fields are aligned with the polarities in the same direction, we could be expelled as our south/north poles flip. So it is a fascinating time for those of us studying astrophysics."

John just stared at his hand and feet moving them under his x-ray vision and marveling and imagining how superman must feel to see this. This was so cool, in a weird sort of way. Abruptly it was over. John now looked at Travis with a new sense of appreciation but did have one question. "Why, if you know all this, are you coming on this trip with us?"

Travis laughed. "I have no family, being one of those orphaned foster children lost in the welfare system, so no attachments to anyone to go home to during the break. Without graduating first, I can't play an important or active role in my field with the government. So, I am at loose ends right now; this looks like the best place to be on a research team uncovering the ancient secrets to the biggest astrological question of our time. After all, with this, there is no place to hide, and with my knowledge, I just might be able to save your butt," he said, slapping John on the back and jabbing him in the shoulder for good measure.

John looked over at Travis, noticing for the first time that Travis was dressed sharp, mussed up from sleeping in his clothes, but definitely not casual. He looked to be about the same size, except Travis looked like he spent a lot of time out in the Hawaii surf during the day when he was not watching the stars by night. To stay in shape here on campus, John had resorted to the body-building gym, which broadened his shoulders, arms, and thighs while tightening his belly. His body did not have the panther tone of Travis's body. John asked as he started to rummage through his closet, "What do you have for work clothes, such as the type you will need on an archeological site?"

Travis shook his head. "Sorry, traveled light, with one professional suit, and the rest summer casual," he said, lifting up a colorful Hawaiian shirt out of the backpack for John to see.

"Well, you are going to need a hat," he said, tossing a dusty brown battered, weathered khaki fedora, so worn that it could pass for an oilcloth. "You will be amazed at just how cold desert nights can get," he added, tossing Travis a jacket made of what Travis could only venture to guess was made out of canvas material. It had an earthy feel to it, and upon trying it on found it to be surprisingly comfortable, light and with a bi-swing back relaxed for easy movement fit. Loaded with pockets, this jacket was made for adventure. "You have any jeans?" John asked, his voice floating up from the depths of his closet as the left hand threw out a couple of pairs, which Travis caught. "One last thing, what size are your feet, cause dress shoes where we are going is not going to work."

Travis nodded. "Size 11's," he said, looking at his feet.

"Then you are going to love these; I have never found boots to be comfortable straight out of the box. They were so good I bought three more just like them."

Throwing boots, brand new straight out of the box, at Travis as he grabs a few items of his own to throw in his backpack for the trip.

"Hey, I appreciate all this, but can't I just go out and pick up what I need as we go?" Travis was used to traveling light as he stuffed what he could into his backpack.

"It is hard to find stuff in our sizes over in the Middle East," John said. "I am going to make the flight arrangements, and if we have to, we will fly standby; we need to get ready now. We will be stopping by my father's place to get it more secure and cleaned up for the next break and enter. You find that you will have a harder time getting in." Gave Travis a punch in the shoulder, letting him know he was kidding.

Quickly details were worked out over the phone with the airline, and John and Travis were soon heading out the door. John snapped his fingers as he remembered there was one other thing he wanted to get out of his father's place before taking off, "Remind me to grab the translation book," he said, not even looking in Travis's direction as he threw all the backpacks in the back seat.

When they arrived at his father's place, it wasn't only a few minutes later that the repairmen came in to change the locks and repair the window. After paying them, John remembered to grab the translation book and the copy of Hezron's journal. He held an empty cardboard box and swished all the perishables out of the refrigerator into it. He knew a homeless person down the street who would appreciate it.

Unbeknownst to them, Karen was watching them come and go from the building. She tried to get a good look at their faces as they went by. The driver could identify as the Professor's son, and she had no idea who the other was.

John stopped on the street corner three blocks down and hollered at the vagrant pushing a cart, "Hey, are you hungry?" The vagrant stopped and grinned.

It was his buddy from the mission. "Hey, John, what are you doing?"

Digging into the trunk of his car, John pulled out the box and said," Going on a trip and will not be needing this. Think you could use it?"

"Sure, thanks," he said, taking the box out of John's hand and putting it into his grocery cart. "You travel safely now, ya hear?" the vagrant hollered as John's car maneuvered back into the traffic and was gone.

Being about the same age, once John and Travis settled into their seats for the long flight, the sense of adventure began to become realized, and soon they were talking about other things they had in common to pass the time away. They discovered that they rooted for the same football teams and were both racquetball players. They talked about girls and parties they had been to and the hilarious things that occurred. The flight was long, and the 'getting-to-know-you' conversation ate up the travel time.

In what seemed like hardly any time, they were so caught in a conversation that they were in the Paris International Airport waiting for a connecting flight. News of the weather conditions and how they affected flights were reflected on the arrival and departure boards, with canceled and delay notifications. The airlines were not flying if any atmospheric storms were expected. These storms had taken down numerous planes because of instrumental failures, and John and Travis's flight had been lucky, but it just wasn't safe to fly right now. During the storm lulls, the flights out were booked to the max, and airports were crazy with travelers trying to get to their destinations.

Travis and John decided that since they were in no hurry to catch the next flight, they would take the airline's offer of accommodations and the next flights out tomorrow. The airline generously offered them enough money for an evening's meal to go along with the package deal. They would see if they could catch a flight the following day and spend the night checking out the night spots of gay Paree 'as they elbowed each other over the beautiful female form before them. With a bit of extra cost, the tickets were exchanged for the next day's flight to Alexandra, and they quickly headed out the door for a night on the town. The first stop was food and a nice restaurant where they could experience the exquisite French cuisine. Hailing a taxi, they tipped him to choose the most excellent French restaurant he suggested.

It wasn't that much further when they came across an open-air café and stopped there to eat. Two local good-looking young females were sitting at the table next to theirs, and soon they were introducing themselves, and it didn't take much to convince the ladies to join them. The girls spoke English fluently, much to Travis and John's relief. These girls were from England and attended the French Art school down the street. They volunteered to show them a nightclub after they finished eating.

Travis nudged John with a smile as he eyed the dark-eyed beauty beside him. John agreed as he grinned at the shapely brunette beside him. With wine flowing, the conversation was followed by laughter, jokes, ribbings, and flirting. On into the night, they talked until the sidewalk café closed. Arm in arm, they drifted down the street towards the nightclub. High winds and heavy rain broke out upon them violently and suddenly threw them forward. Heavy white sheets of rain whipped down like blankets thrown on the bed. Each blanket of rain was whiting out everything, including the street and buildings before them. Travis and John were both able to shelter the girls under their arms as they made their way to the nightclub door. They were soaked and windblown but thankfully under shelter. Just as suddenly as it started, it quit. Shaking the water off, laughingly, they entered the nightclub.

Chapter 8

After arriving in Cairo, James headed to a hotel, dropped off his bags, rented a car, and headed out to see an old friend of his, Professor Ques Adana, from his college days. Ques was born in the area and had studied the Qessim as a child. Ques were familiar with the local terrain and would likely have a better knowledge of the site's history. They both loved the ancient world of the Middle East. The only difference between the two was that Ques was a Christian and was looking to use such information to prove his faith, while James was interested in it all for the academic historical setting.

James already had it on his agenda to include the River bac d'Abu Safar that encircled this land where Hezron was last known to possess the parchment in his travels. This land was known as "the other side of the river Kush," and Professor Goldberg was on an archeological dig in the area. James figured that if anyone knew what happened to the people and the area during that time, it would be the Professor.

The decline of Kush is a hotly debated topic, and James and Ques got into the reasons for the varying reasons for its decline during a lunch break at a seminar in Italy. James knew that Ques was a very knowledgeable man on the religious history of the area and wondered if the man knew more about Hezron, who, according to legend, was raised in the area.

Ques was home with his wife and two children having dinner when James arrived. They invited him in to have dinner with them. Enjoying a home-cooked meal, and resting in the light entertainment of children and their adventures of the day, Ques and James teased and quizzed the children regarding their knowledge of world history and biblical history. They seem to have a good understanding of the civilization that came from the Old Testament, where Cush was one of the sons of Ham.

After the children were excused from the table, James got down to the reason for his visit. "You know that I have been researching middle age writers who had studied the Hezron's narratives and how they were divided in their opinions concerning the truth of the parchments and the prophecies contained within."

"Yes, I have been following your work closely through the *Archeology Today* when you get around to writing a piece for it," Ques said.

"The biggest things were Hezron accurately writing about what happened in his journal, which I believe is one of the greatest findings I have put together so far. Much of what I know is because of the manuscript journal of Hezron," James explained.

"Yes, his journals have been tied to many events that occurred in the region and during that time period. It has been placed in the same eye witnessing category as Josephus works," Ques acknowledged.

"One critic saw him as a Karate missionary endeavoring to discredit the Talmud regarding the proper way to slaughter." James dug up and started rummaging through the papers he brought to go over.

Ques leaned back, bemused. "Some aspects of the story are very accurate. For example, the halakhot, which is the proper way to examine and slaughter animals according to Hezron, is genuine and still in use among the countrymen of Ethiopia."

"You have confirmed what I have been suspicious of for a long time. Kind of knew that you would know exactly where this type of kosher slaughter came from," he said, smiling with relief at his friend's knowledge and understanding. James brought out another document with those papers shuffled back in his satchel. "Others regarded Hezron as a mere charlatan whose sayings and doings are not worth attention. Still, others outright denied the existence of Hezron and considered the documents forgeries. What do you think?"

Ques looked at James with one eye closed. "Are you starting to doubt yourself and your ability to discern the difference?"

"Truth be told, I believe that the nature of his book reads like a historical novel in which the truth is mixed with imagination making it greater in its storytelling. I have to verify everything to separate that which is fanciful from that which is factual. You have answered one aspect, which I thank you for. I know you are an authority on this subject, and I trust your judgment. It is one of the reasons for this......." James never finished his sentence.

A rock came crashing through the window and was soon followed by a Molotov cocktail. The fiery cocktail flamed across the carpet and up the curtains. Loud hard banging echoed through the front door. The door creaked and groaned under pressure but did not give. Tremendous noise outside, a tumult of voices in angry tones called out insults to Ques, his faith, and his family.

The children ran to their father, and the wife stood wide-eyed in fear. Ques quickly pushed them towards the upstairs, where they raced to the roof. Ques, along with his wife, grabbed different articles as they ran, shouting at James to follow quickly. James and Ques quickly passed the children out the top floor window to the roof that ran along to the next roof only a few feet apart. Tossing the children from one roof to the other, they quickly got everyone across to the next top. They covered two more roofs before they came to a hillside as high as the roof, and from there, they headed to a parked car.

Ques was obviously prepared with an escape route should they encounter any hostilities at home. James applauded Ques's foresight but wondered why to stay where it was not safe for the children. Piling in and gunning the motor, they were soon on their way out. Getting a few blocks down the road, James turned to keep a watch to see if anyone was following. Glancing in the rearview mirror, James spotted a van quickly catching up with them.

Turning the city streets into a race track, the two vehicles were near missing people on the roads and dodging other cars as they weaved in and out of traffic. Ques looked very determined as his wife and children were huddled in the backseat, praying and crying. Ques quickly told James, "I have been receiving death threats lately at work and even to my wife and children at home because of our faith. It used to be individual sporadic and isolated. This is not unusual in this part of the world," he said as he swerved to miss a pedestrian crossing the street. "Lately, we have heard from the experiences of others. If we are caught by some of the jihad factions, our life will be over. There have now arisen factions that make sure that it would be a violent and prolonged slow torturous death."

"Aren't the police doing anything about this?" James asked.

"It used to be that we would get a little appeasement effort, but now it is just a blind eye on these matters. We knew it was serious enough to have a contingency plan for just such an event," Ques said as he rounded a corner on two wheels, scaring everyone in the car.

With hands on the ceiling and window and his feet pushing through the floor mat, James, anchored himself, said, "So why not leave before this?"

"My professorship at the local University pays well," Ques said with a shrug as he continued to weave in and out of traffic, firmly gripping the steering wheel while frantically looking for openings in traffic ahead. "I had left the car up on the hillside ridge just in case, trained my children to be always prepared, and while now I am glad I did, I think putting you all in this kind of danger was not worth it," he said as he drove the car through a vegetable vendor's cart full of cabbages. "Right now, I am very determined to get away from these people."

Gunfire was now spraying the back of his car, and he swerved left and right, trying to decrease the accuracy of their fire. His wife and children were crouched down as low as they could go and tossed left and right as the car continued to fly down the road.

James remembered road construction that he passed by on the way to Ques' home and suggested, "Turn left now. Turn a very sharp right immediately to avoid the road construction." But it was too late as Ques broke through the barrier, raced through the construction site, and made a very sharp right into a nearby alleyway. The car following them couldn't make the turn and drifted in a spray of rocks and dirt into the road construction site hole. Ques looked behind him to see that the van was no longer following them. He gave a sigh of relief and slowed down.

With that, Ques declared after reassuring himself that they were no longer being followed. "We were going to Mahalla to be with my brother. James, I can drop you off where ever you like, or you can come with us. My brother has something that might be of interest to you, and I am not sure it is safe for you to stay here as you have now been identified as having been with me." Ques eased up on the gas and, with a bit of shifting of his weight in the seat, relaxed his knuckle-white grip on the steering wheel. Then taking each hand in turn, flexed the circulation back into the fingers.

"Let me help with the gas." The relief on their faces said that he was more than welcome. "Could you stop at my hotel so I can pick up my luggage? It won't take but a minute since I have not yet unpacked." From there, he called the car rental agency and notified them where they would find their car. He gathered up his luggage, and off they went to Mahalla.

Mahalla was where the Jewish Orthodox Church claimed to have the biblical Ark of the Covenant and the tables of the law where the Ten Commandments were inscribed. James figured it wouldn't hurt to visit the church in the area if it was safe to do so.

The children were soon soothed and fast asleep in their mother's arms as Ques and James whispered in the front seat. "I was certain that the parchment Hezron carried with him exists, and if I find it, it will be considered one of this century's greatest finds. Did you know I have now got my son involved in this research, and I am tickled that John is willing to go to a Jewish theology seminary? He will learn anything that might pertain to the culture, folklore, and religious understanding of both the period in which Hezron lived and the period I think the parchment may have come out of. I am hoping my son would come up with something to tie in with his studies at the university so that it doesn't take too time away from his academic work."

"You sound like a father. How do you like it?" Ques asked.

"Strange! After all these years of learning, I have a grown son. What is more exciting is that he is the son I have always wanted," James acknowledged proudly. James settled in for the long drive. "Not to change the subject, but I have been meaning to ask. Do you have any knowledge of Hezron?"

"The only thing that I know that you have not mentioned is Hezron was supposed to have possessed a parchment that came from the Queen Makeda, according to one legend. She was supposed to have written all the things Solomon had taught her. She was there during her visit to Jerusalem as a representative of her country Sheba. At least, that is how tradition tells the story. During that time, she gave birth to her son Menelik who assumed the throne and inherited the parchment after her death. According to the legend that I know, it was the son who brought home the Ark of the covenant after meeting with his father in Jerusalem," Ques said with a half smile. "In my own family, we link ourselves to the half of the Jews who follow the law of Moses and who have Menelik's royal blood running through our veins on our mother's side." Then Ques went on to say, "What Solomon did was send one son of each of his nobles and one son of each of the temple priests with Menelik when he returned to his kingdom. He had a replica made of the Ark for them to take with them, but the son of Zadok, the High Priest, secretly switched the replica with the real Ark and brought it into Ethiopia, where it remains to this day. At least, that is what we tell our kids. And that has been passed down through the family for generations."

"What else can you tell me about the parchment?" James quizzed Ques.

"What I know of the parchment was it contained the Holiness Code, sections of the Torah, the song of Moses, and the timetable of the galaxy, or at least that is what I understand, and it is according to the legend. The other thing I know was that those who owned it were affected by the words contained within. The prophecies always seem to be read just before they came to pass, as described in the parchment. It was so powerful that when Shama Muhammed thrust the Muslim faith on the people, he soon realized that it was not the people he had to contend with but God. On his deathbed, he prayed full of repentance and told his followers, ' Leave the Abyssinians in peace as long as they do not take offense,' and that about sums it up." Ques smiled as he watched James make notes of this conversation.

"It could be. I will have to keep this under my hat and see if there is any more evidence that would give credence that there is any relationship." James added this to his notes. "More study will have to be given. Send me what you have to get me started once I get back to the States."

"Sure, once I get an opportunity to put it together for you." Ques slowed down as he looked further up the road.

It was a long, dusty road full of military checkpoints and patrolled by vehicles loaded with the gun-bearing militia. A few times, if it wasn't for the smooth handshake of money from James, they would not have been unable to continue and maybe even killed as they saw one car load experience.

One stop at a small village for fuel and food, and back on the road they went hoping to get to Ques's brother's place before morning. James drove most of the night so that Ques could get some rest. This part of the trip was a quiet drive. The stillness of the desert and the openness of the flat terrain spread out before his eyes. Northern lights danced low on the horizon, and in such vibrant colors, James felt blessed to be the one to see them. Everyone else was asleep, and he thought it best to let them sleep. Reflecting on the day, James realized that whatever information Ques had, it wasn't as crucial as first thought. Ques suggest that he go visit a church where Ques's cousin works and see if James knew he would honor Ques's request to see what his brother had.

It was early morning when James pulled to the side of the road and woke Ques. He said, "We are just outside of Mahalla, and I think it would be best if you drove the rest of the way," as he got out of the car to go around to the passenger side.

Chapter 9

Calling Karen, Sam jumped right with, "I think I have lost the Professor. He was visiting his friend when they got hit by the local welcoming committee. I didn't see them leave the building. When the van left in an all-fired hurry, I thought I would see the Professor emerge from his hiding place. "It didn't take me long to figure out that the van had gone and given chase." Turning left, he turned his car around and saw the van at a stop. All the occupants were hollering at a vendor to move his cart off the road. "Do you have any ideas where the Professor could be heading from here?" he said, looking at the blocked road.

"Was he last seen with Ques?" asked Karen.

"Yes, and he left his rental car at Ques's home, but the rental people did not know where he went. Is there any movement on his credit card?"

"If you go to Benes Coffee shop beside the marketplace, there was a man by the name of Gershon who will sell information for a price and seemed to have a knack for knowing what was happening in Cairo. I will call you if I find any activity on the credit card."

Sam asked Karen, "How did you know about Gershon?"

"As a CIA agent, we assemble more than information. We amass contacts in many countries, who are counted on to garner the information for us, for a price," Karen reminded him.

Sam headed down to the marketplace and asked around for Gershon. Finally, at a little café in the corner of the market, the waiter said he knew of such a fellow. He usually came by every evening for a meal, and at that time, he could talk to him. Pressing him with questions, Sam gave the slip of the welcoming moneyed handshake, and with that, the waiter pointed to Gershon's home up on the second floor of a building down the street kitty-corner to the water fountain in the courtyard. The waiter described what Gershon looked like.

With that, Sam was heading off to see if he could find Gershon. Just his luck; a man fitted the description. Gershon was now leaving the building. Running to catch up with him, he called out, "Gershon."

Gershon turned around and looked suspiciously at this stranger running towards him, out of breath and gasping.

Sam mentally reminded himself that he needed to get in better shape. This is ridiculous to be out of breath on a short run, two blocks uphill, and to be wheezing like this as he leaned forward with hands on his knees, trying to catch his breath. Gershon's face morphed from suspicious to incredulous. Who was this American?

When Sam finally got his breath back, he gave the code name Karen had given him. Gershon quickly whisked him inside the building and up the stairs to his room, where they sat in his living room. Gershon quietly assessed this man before him in his room and waited until Sam started explaining what he knew and how he knew the code name.

Sam explained that he was given the name by a retired CIA agent now working for him in the private sector. He explained that Gershon was given high marks for accurate information and went on to say what he was looking for.

Gershon took this all into consideration and told Sam the price. Sam choked on the water offered him and requested a moment while he contacted his client. What really surprised Sam was that amount didn't even cause a blink when he put his request in after explaining what happened, but there was also the warning, "No pay would be coming his way if he failed to find the Professor." He was beginning to think he was not charging enough for this work as he hung up the phone.

Once the deal was settled and half the money was transferred to the account Gershon indicated, he was gone leaving Sam to pace the floors. Sam looked across the city from Gershon's window, wondering why he was even here, when suddenly the sky lit up with a massive fireworks display. Everyone was running into the streets, pointing and watching as the fireworks went off way up in the upper atmosphere for the next ten minutes. The TV in the room went to static, and the lights flickered in the room and across the city. Over the city, there was an explosion as some buildings burst into one colossal fireball. Sam wasn't sure if it was some military strike, some terrorist act, or this electrical static in the air was causing all these problems. He watched in fascination as it played out before his eyes.

Sam called Karen just as soon as the phone was back up and working after the fireworks were over. "Hey, Karen, I have to ask, are you experiencing strange weather over your way? We got exploding buildings, everything electrical shutting down, and lots of static in the air."

Karen said, "The news back here in the US is talking about some eleven-year solar cycle is causing a similar problem over here.

He returned to business and asked her, "Have you had any time to check James' credit cards to see if there has been any recent activity and where? Could I have you check the address where James was last seen and find out who that fellow is and more about him?" The more he thought about it, the more he kicked himself in the butt for not thinking of this before. He should have been getting Karen to check on that fellow sooner, like while he was sitting outside in the car waiting for James to leave.

Thinking back to the screeching of the car's tires beside him outside of the house where he had last seen the Professor. He was really caught napping and was wakened when the self-appointed Muslim militia started pouring out of the back of the van. All he did was hunker down, hoping not to be noticed. These guys were nasty. There must have been about eight of them, and they were loaded for bear. They moved swiftly and noisily, seemly not afraid that anyone was going to stop them. The leader, who was barking out orders, may have been enjoying his position of authority, but even Sam could tell this man was lacking in military or law enforcement procedures. All his men rushed to the front door and were raising such a ruckus, waving guns and demanding entrance, that Sam shook his head slightly as he watched from his car.

On command, the self-appointed militia proceeded to bust the door down. After a few attempts by the militia to beat the door down with shoulders and then feet, one of them had the brilliant idea to shoot the lock, almost injuring the fellow whose hand was on the knob at the time. With some cursing and several more rounds at the safety, the door finally gave way, and they poured in, shooting as they went.

Sam could see through the window curtains movement as they searched the house, and he could hear more curses as they poured out of the house towards the van. Scrambling back into the truck, they u-turned and lurched away as the driver shifted gears. Smoke billowed out the back as it worked up some speed. Sam kind of half chuckled to himself as he turned his car around and followed at a safe distance.

What in the world did the Professor or his friend do to spark such a problem. Sam's reminiscing was interrupted by the cell phone ringing. Gershon's voice came over the other end, "My sources tell me his name is Professor Ques Adana, whom the Professor had gone to university with." The address was correct, but now the information was a little old unless Gershon was holding back and knew more about this Ques.

It didn't take long before Gershon was back in the room. "I will look further and see what else I can find out if you wish," he said and gave Sam that look of 'nothing more until I see more money.' Sam gave what he had in his pocket, which seemed to satisfy Gershon.

With Karen and Gershon working on who and what connections this Professor Ques Adana had, maybe Sam will be able to have it a little easier to keep track of Professor Holden. So far, Gershon seemed to be a leech and one lousy snitch. He decided that Gershon probably would not be a good source. Leaving the building, he was definitely not going to be a source to wait around for more info. Gershon called. "The van you described is over by the road construction on Gahar Street, and you might still catch it if you hurry," he said and then abruptly hung up.

Sam hung up the phone and dug out the map in the car to find out where Gahar Street was before taking off. He arrived at the location to find the van still there. Sam sat in the car thinking about his following options. He was now parked about twenty feet away from the sinkhole that had swallowed up the van. He had driven past the sinkhole to pick up the chase after the Professor. It soon became apparent that they were long gone.

So Sam turned a few times until he returned and was parked where he could watch and see if the van's occupants were having any better luck. They almost had the van out of the sinkhole, but it didn't look like they were going to pursue it anymore. Sam knew they had given up the chase, and the trail had gone cold.

Gershon called back to say without preamble, "neither Professor Ques nor his wife was not from around this area but actually came from Mahalla where his only living brother was currently residing." Gershon suggested that that might be an excellent place to look.

Checking with the map, Sam saw that it would be a bit of a journey, and he might as well gather up his things, calling Karen to let her know of his plans. He couldn't get through and, after several attempts, gave up. Checking his watch, saw that it would soon be morning and decided to let her sleep for a few hours before making the call. Sam turned on the car as he meandered out towards Mahalla. It was a long and uneventful trip.

Halfway, he called Karen again and this time got through, "Gershon was able to give me some information on Ques, and since I have no other leads, I am heading to Mahalla, hoping that Professor James went with them. How is it going at your end?"

Karen said, "Since last night, I am resolved on getting my camera back or at the very least the memory card out of it. I might be able to call a friend that works in the police department and see if he wouldn't mind taking the memory card out of the camera that is currently in evidence. I will be getting back to you when I learn more."

She hated to involve more people in this, but since she didn't know if the pics were worth the crime of another break and enter, she voted for extraction from the police department if it was possible. This whole case was getting to be more trouble than it was worth in her eyes, and she was really beginning to wonder what all the hoopla was about.

Laying in bed, Karen thought back over the last couple of years, allowing her mind to wander and sort things out in a manner that usually worked well for her. Up to now, Sam had been doing primarily easy surveillance in the States, and this was the first international case they had been in a long time since forming the partnership. So far, this case was just a matter of following Professor Holden and whatever he was after and maybe getting it from him, given Sam's undercover story. She didn't like the idea of the international border transportation of stolen goods, but given that they were not required to handle that, it did ease somewhat her mind. Being in the spy business all these years, transporting information across lines was not so big a hop, skip and jump from what they were doing right now, except it didn't sit quite right. It clicked. She needed to learn who was, behind the curator in the museum, financing this little project. But first, she needed her stuff back.

Jumping out of bed, her stiff and sore joints creaked in protest. Slowing the pace, she walked over to the kitchen to get the coffee going, the kinks out, back to the bathroom to get the shower going, and brush her teeth. It didn't take long before she was dressed, coffee in hand, and out the door to start another day.

Heading to the precinct, she concocted a likely tale of the theft in her mind. Entering the police precinct, she took in the hustle and bustle, the faint dirty air of unkempt bodies of the unfortunates who frequently were booked and incarcerated amid the physical testosterone of patrol officers who held the air of superiority about themselves. She was a breath of fresh air to the room, and a welcome sight to the men looking at her as she, with confidence born from years of working in such an environment, could portray. With all eyes on her, the officers appreciated taking a break from the drudgery of daily routine. They watched her come up to the counter to explain why she was there. Many men had given her the twenty-one gun salute for her charisma and feminine perfection.

As polished as a lawyer on a mission, she presented the need to speak to an officer. "Who is the homicide detective on the murder case of John Horton? May I speak with him, please?"

The officer, at the receiving window, recovering from his tongue hanging to the floor. Checking his notes, and pointed to the door. "You will need to see Lieutenant Millar. Third door down on your right," he said as the security locked unlocked with its annoying buzz.

At the appropriate office, she found a familiar face. "Detective Millar," she declared sweetly with a quick change of persona, giving her old classmate a generous hug in front of all her peers. A delight to see his old classmate, he was more than elated to have her come to visit him, much to the envy of his fellow detectives, plus giving him a break from the paperwork before him. They chatted for a few moments about how life had been since they last saw each other and finally got down to the reason for her visit.

"I was working a case when I was attacked on Chester Street. I was taking some pictures. The thugs attacked me as I was about to re-enter my car. I was robbed of the contents of my purse, and the camera was taken. I really don't wish to press charges at this time, but on listening in on the police radio band, I found out that it wasn't a short time later that a bunch were arrested for the murder of John Horton. I understand that you are on the case."

"That's correct, so what can I do for you?" Detective Millar asked.

"Was there a Nikon D90, color black, among the articles retrieved from the gang recently arrested?" Karen asked.

"Let me look at the report. Give me a moment to check." Millar turned to the file before him and, upon a few flips of the pages, found the list of articles, one of which was the Nikon D90. "Yep, nice camera, kind of thought it might have been stolen. Do you want to file a report?"

"Could you do me this favor, after all the hours I put into helping you study for your finals? As a favor for old time sake?" she asked, her eyes pleading. "I do not want it to jeopardize the case I'm working on, nor add to yours. All I really need is the memory card," she said, pausing just long enough to give him a chance to mull over the request before continuing. "You will find that I have the camera with my name etched on the inside battery lid, and if you want, you can return it after your case is closed. I would appreciate it," she said, smiling sweetly.

"I will make you a deal. Identify the men involved in this assault from pictures that fit the description you have given us of the assailants, and I will see what I can do for you. Deal?" she asked, holding out her hand.

"Deal," Karen said as she shook his hand.

The Detective looked around to check who might be listening in. At the admiration of his fellow detectives, who seemed oblivious to the conversation, he smiled. They were far enough away that all they were doing was visualizing some hormonal-driven body search, he guessed by the look of their faces. He turned back to her and nodded.

"Could you wait here just one moment, please?" He returned shortly with a description of the camera on the list and the evidence box number assigned to the case. He asked her to come down with him to the Evidence Room, and he might have found her camera. "Come with me," he said, taking the vision of loveliness away from the view of the other detectives. He was glad to get her all to himself before they came with excuses, snooping around his desk. She followed him down to the basement and down the long hallway to the last door on the right. They entered a room caged away from where all the stored evidence was kept. Leading the way, he took her to the Evidence Room and asked for Case #241FC.

The Detective signed for the evidence, and together they looked through the articles taken, and after inspection, she declared that it was her camera. In the box, he withdrew the camera and, upon checking the battery lid, did find her name there. Made a note on the box that once the case is closed, return the camera to the address she gave him. Retrieving the memory card for her. He looked at the pics on the camera and saw that they were not related to his case and handed them over to her.

He directed her to another officer who, under strict instructions from Detective Millar, was expedient in taking down all the information she had on the assailants and their attack and theft. She told them of how she was down on Chester Street doing a little investigation, taking pictures, when these thugs came and ganged up on her, shoved her into the alley where they proceeded to rob the contents of her purse. He jotted down all the information and informed her that she would need to see if she could identify her assailants. She signed the report as accurate and true to her recollection.

The radio playing soft music in the background crackled in the corner of the robbery division room, with a brief interruption of the regularly scheduled program for a news flash. "We are sorry to interrupt your regularly scheduled program to bring this latest update on our atmospheric weather conditions. Due to the recent hit of X-ray flare, the earth has experienced a global expansion of the gases in the atmosphere, and there will be a heat wave to follow over the next few days. Please be advised to stay indoors with food rations and plenty of water. We are not sure how much interference with our electrical and communication systems we will experience or how bad they will be affected at this time. More auroras are expected, and the expanding atmosphere may encroach on the satellites' orbits which could drop them out of their orbital positions. Stay tuned for more minute-by-minute, up-to-date information in our broadcasts. This is George Brown, KNGM, your atmospheric weatherman reporting to you live. Now back to our regularly scheduled program."

Everyone in the room paused whatever they were doing to listen in, and Karen listened with avid attention. After the report was over, there was some discussion about it, but it wasn't long before it was business as usual in the office.

Later as she was about to get into her car, Detective Millar came over. He noticed earlier the lock pick and asked, "I have to ask you, was that lock pick yours?" The air went static, and with hair rising up, the door handle of her car gave her a big enough shock to make her yelp and shake her fingers.

Detective Millar was all attentive. "Are you ok?" he asked, grabbing her fingers to examine.

She pondered whether to tell him it was hers or not as she licked the tips of her fingers to take the sting off. "Oh, the fingers will be fine." She decided that since the chances of her being discovered breaking into the Professor's place was remote, it would be ok to declare that the lockpick was hers. She opened up her tool kit to visual check before her friend on the pick's status and nodded. "Yes, looks like they could be mine."

He asked, "Then why didn't you declare it earlier."

She shrugged it off. "I didn't realize it was missing," she said, getting into her car.

Detective Millar took a step forward and, leaning up against the car as casually as he could, asked, "Hey, I have to ask. Are you attached or currently seeing anyone?"

"No," she said and smiled sincerely. "You know me, nose to the grindstone." Karen turned on the car and put it into reverse, thankful that Millar had been lenient with her and allowed her the memory card. She profusely thanked him. "Listen, I am really grateful for your help. Here is my business card should you ever need my help with a case," she said, handing over the card. On her way out, she added, "We will have to get together some time, as I owe you a drink or at least a lunch." With a wave out her window, she headed towards the exit.

She didn't slow down and let the conversation linger. Buying lunch was the least she could offer an old friend for his help, but that was it. Besides, she thought to herself, that should take his mind off of the pick and the implications. Breathing a sigh of relief as she left the police department's parking lot, she called Sam to let him know of her success. She looked in her rearview mirror to see Millar standing there watching her leave.

Getting back to the office, she quickly loaded its memory onto the computer. Grabbing another cup of coffee, she sat at the computer to take a look at the pictures. It was blank. She was sure that she had taken the pictures. So what happened. This was incredible. How could the photos have been erased? A magnet was the only thing she could think of to do such a thing. But where did it come in contact with a magnet? This mystified Karen. She reflected on all the static on her car when she entered it earlier. Could that be enough to erase all the pictures? She knew the photos were on the camera when she and Detective Millar looked at them together in the Evidence Room. So, where did they go? This whole case was now beginning to exasperate her. With Sam having problems keeping track of one Professor, now she can't even get some pictures without a lot of aggravation. This case was not running smoothly.

When the phone rang, Karen picked up on the first ring. The curator was on the other end asking, "When are you going to bring over the pictures of the documents?" Sam must have informed him, and now she was going to have to stall for time while she figured out a way to get another copy.

"I will bring over what I have by this evening," she said. After hanging up with the curator, she reluctantly called Sam back to let him know the latest news. Sam told her that she needed to get pictures of the document because the curator had called him, also indicating that he was a little put out with the lack of forthcoming evidence.

After getting off the phone, Karen headed to the local camera shop to pick up another camera that would take the same memory card and stopped off at the electronic store specializing in surveillance equipment. Getting another lock pick, she headed to the Professor's place, hoping that no one was there.

Chapter 10

It didn't take Ques long to reach his brother's house. The brothers hugged, and the women stood behind their men and watched. The children hid behind their mothers and silently took it all in.

Ques turned to James and brought him forward. "Let me introduce you to an old classmate of mine, Dr. James Holden. James, let me introduce you to my brother, Mohaim Adana."

"Mohaim offered a seat to James and said, "Come, come sit. Any friend of my brother is a friend of the family." Soon the women and children were shooed out of the living room so the men could talk.

Ques explained to his brother, "James is interested in a fourth-century man by the name of Hezron who was known in this region for his knowledge, wisdom, and having a scroll from the Alexandria library."

His brother asked James, "What exactly are you looking for? How much do you know about this Hezron?" The ladies brought in tea and sweets for the guests and then sat discreetly behind the wall to watch the interchange. On hearing the extensive knowledge, he had of Hezron and his travels, Mohaim felt better about telling him, "There is the tribe of Jews that used to live in the area, which could be the tribe where Hezron came from." Scarcely had he started to talk when the children ran through the room, giggling and playing until Ques clapped his hands to get their attention and shooed them out.

Mohaim brought James up to speed. "Actually, the Jewish community today is led by an energetic woman. She has kept the Jewish community alive with all her organized social activities with the women in her community, and she hopes to regain our church property and restore it again as a synagogue. She is working extensively to save the local Jewish cemetery, and I believe she might be able to tell you more. She has extensive knowledge of the Jewish presence from the time the Jews lived in Egypt to the present day. Maybe we can set up a meeting with her for you."

"Not this trip. I have a son heading my way, and I am supposed to meet him in Jerusalem soon. Maybe next time," James said, graciously turning down the invitation.

"Well, she knows where some important documents that attest to the early Jewish life in Egypt come from the papers found in the Geniza. This early work complained of the soldiers of Darius destroying their temple. In case you don't know, the word Geniza means funeral, where any documents or books bearing the name of God are buried. It is forbidden by their religion to tear or burn anything that bears His name," Mohaim explained.

"So you think that what I am looking for may be among these documents?" James quizzed.

"Can't say, but I can tell you that a considerable amount of documents were found by chance in the 1800s in one of the chambers of the Synagogue. Most of the documents from the Middle Ages were given to Cambridge University," Morhaim said.

Ques piped in. "The church that he is the pastor over was once a synagogue, and in the back, there is a floor with an interesting mosaic design that you might be interested in looking at."

Mohaim went on to describe it. "There are circles within circles and a pattern of animals and hieroglyphs I was unfamiliar with encircling the mosaic. There is a blood red moon or sun, but I am not sure which," he admitted with a shrug.

As Mohaim described the mosaic pattern and drew it out on paper, the more excited James became. 'Now you have my interest," James admitted. With what Travis said on the phone about a blood-red moon and its relationship to the feasts, it could well be that Travis might be on the right track in deciphering the meaning of the mosaic relief Mohaim was now describing.

"Tomorrow morning, we can go to the Synagogue and take a look. Tonight you must dine with us." The conversation turned to food, from the wonderful smell wafting in from the kitchen as the women scurried to bring it out onto the table. Soon they were gathered around the table, enjoying good food and company as brothers and family members got caught up on the latest events that brought them together.

Mohaim convinced his brother that he and his family should not return to their home but set up with them until they could find work and another home to live in. Mohaim invited James aside after supper because there was something that he wanted to discuss with him. Mohaim asks him, "Did you have anything to do with the raid on my brother's place?"

"No, no, absolutely not," both Ques and James replied, and after much assurance from both men, Mohaim came to believe that James was not the cause of his brother's house raid. Once re-assured that James just happened to be visiting from the US with his brother when Ques' house was raided, Mohaim gave James a big hug of friendship and asked for forgiveness.

Later that evening, James bid them goodnight and headed out the door to find a hotel, even with protests still ringing in his ears to stay. James knew their house was overflowing with both of their families and politely declined.

James was pointed to the local bed and breakfast. It was the guest home of one of Mohaim's friends not far down the street from where Mohaim lived. It was a clean, small, quiet room. There was a communal kitchen where James could prepare his own meals if he wished, or he could have meals prepared for him. It was like a home away from home for him. Palm trees outside his window gently rustled with the breeze. The fan slowly rotated to gently encourage the evening air to come into his room. James was soon settled into a place where he could shower, change and work quietly into the night. Thinking over the day's events, he reviewed the information he had received. That reminded him that John's newfound friend, Travis gave him a whole new line of thought that looked like it might be on the right track. Thinking about the boys, James decided to call his son to see how their flight was, as they should be arriving in Alexandria any time now if they haven't already arrived.

Chapter 11

Sam called Karen and asked, "Could you do a little research on Professor Ques and see what some of his dissertations were about?"

Karen was already ahead of him and quickly reported, "Ques mainly focused on research concerning scripture. He is of the Ethiopian branch of the Christian faith, which means their bible has a couple more books than the ones we were used to. It seemed his focus was on The Book of Jubilees and Enoch. He was out to prove they were worthy of being included in the canon as they contained great truths that could be proven by archeology. One of the premises he was working on was that the Book of Jubilees talks about Enoch commanding a tabernacle to be built in Salem."

"Yeah, that sort of fits what the Professor was indicating when he talked about his friend," Sam acknowledged. "Anything else?"

"Ahh, yes, there is. Using a pivoting point of Psalms 76:2, Ques relates how it is the same place where the tabernacle was built in Jerusalem. Another part of the premise is that the original order of faith was that of Melchizedek at Salem, better known in his book as "Order of Tzedek," a priestly order from which the Aaronic order sprang. Hold on a minute while I get that information," Karen said as she looked for it amid all the papers on her desk.

"Do you think it is important to what Professor Holden is researching?" Sam asked.

"Not exactly, but some aspects may be valuable to Professor Holden's current research. In Ques's book, he makes a lot of references to the Mishnah. For example, when running from Esau, Jacob finds sanctuary in the order of Malki-Tzedek, where he is taught the Torah. I do not know if this is of any interest to you, but I did pass it on to the curator, who encouraged us to keep digging. From the sounds of his voice, I believe the real trail the curator is on has more to do with this 'Order of Tzedek. And for that reason, I think we should have an interest in how it all relates," Karen deduced.

"Ok, if this Tzedek order crosses my path, my ears will perk up," Sam promised.

"By the way," Karen said, switching subjects, "those fellows going in and out of the Professor's home have been back and have left again. It looks like they may be taking off to make a little trip somewhere. So I do not think we will be seeing them anytime soon. I have not been able to find out much about their identities or purpose as I have been busy with the theft and recapturing the photos. Should I have followed them? Because I just have a feeling they are more important than the photos I took. Woman's intuition, you understand."

Sam said, "Whatever floats your boat. The curator has said nothing to me about following anyone but the Professor in this case."

"I will keep an ear open for any references to this priest line info if I come across it when I search the building again," Karen commented before hanging up the phone. Sam and Karen have always had short and brief discussions over the phone as if they were on the same wavelength.

Karen immediately started digging into the backgrounds of the Professor's son, his friend Ques, and Professor Goldberg so that when she talked with Sam again, she would have the information. Organizing her ever-growing files, in this case, took the next few hours.

A little later, she realized that she had not been out to have lunch. Usually, she and Sam would get together for lunch and discuss whatever ongoing case they were on. Today, she would have to eat alone. She decided to call for Chinese delivery, as she opened her file on delivery menus that she always kept on her desk for such a moment as this. Her thoughts were interrupted by the jarring telephone sound. Ever professional, she picked with her best business voice, "S and K Private Investigators, how may I help you?"

"Hi, Karen, it is me, Steve. I was wondering if I could persuade you to take me out for that lunch you promised?" said Lieutenant Millar crossing his fingers, hoping she would be free and would say yes.

"Hi Steve, you must be on the same wavelength as my stomach. I was just thinking about ordering in a Chinese delivery," she said, tucking the menu back in the file. Karen was all for eating out. After all, she did say she would take him out to lunch, and this was a good time as any to keep her promise. "Where shall we meet? What are you hungry for?" she asked, trying to think of a nice restaurant to go to.

Just then, the floor started to shiver, and articles began sliding off her desk, causing Karen to drop the phone as she went to grab them before they hit the floor. She could catch the desk for support and hold most of the papers to the desk until the quaking was over.

"Hello, hello. Are you still there? Is everything alright?" Steven's voice could be heard coming from the dangling phone.

Karen quickly picked it up and said, "Did you feel that?"

Steven's car had shivered while the earth quaked. With his foot on the brake, he could keep it from rolling down the incline on the street. "Yeah, I felt it. I have not known New York to be a place for earthquakes. It was a small one, and I hope no one is hurt," he said, getting right back on topic. "There does seem to be a lot more of those earthquakes now. But anyway, back to what we were talking about before being rudely interrupted. There is this new place I know. I haven't checked it out yet, but my partner says it is a great little place. We should try it. I thought maybe we could go try it together. Are you free right now?" Steven asked.

"Sure, where do I go to meet you?'

"Down the stairs, I am right outside. You don't mind riding in my patrol car?" Sam answered while reaching down on the passenger side to pick up the fast food cartons on the floor left by his partner and tossing them in the back seat.

"Will be right down," Karen said, hung up, grabbed her coat, and headed out the door.

Chapter 12

Travis and John woke up to a throbbing headache and bloodshot eyes. John was in the bathroom, examining the morning after face, while Travis rolled over in bed, throwing the covers over his head, wishing they didn't have to get going so soon. Their flight would be leaving in about three hours, and it was the first flight out.

"Ugh!" Travis groaned and forced himself up. He struggled to stand up and headed over to get a drink of water and sit on the can, exhausted from the exertion, with jet lag, hung over from the wine, and very little sleep. He felt whooped. After jumping in the shower, Travis was soon revived and ready to roll.

John grabbed the shower next and took the pelting of water on his body as he braced himself against the shower wall, hoping that it would help. He took so long that Travis had to remind him, "Get a move on. We have a plane to catch."

The guys put themselves together and managed to get to the airport just in time for their flight. While waiting for their flight to leave, John's cell rang, and it was his father. Bringing his father up to speed on what had transpired so far and how the flight schedule was working out, John was able to tell his father they were catching a plane within the next few minutes and should be arriving later this evening. The overhead intercom came announcing their flight was now ready for boarding, so John hastily rounded up the phone call with a promise to call when he arrived. By the time they were seated on the plane, they felt a little more like themselves and were again ready to face the world.

Travis approaches John about the Malki-Tzedek order. John explained, "The order established itself as a school to teach then Egypt happened." Leaning over, he added, "Did you know that Jethro, Moses' father-in-law, was a priest of this order?"

Travis said, "No, and this fits how?"

John said, "Why do you think God chose Moses or why two laws, one called the law of Moses, and the other called the Law of God?" he asked, pausing to receive the coffee he ordered from the flight attendant and pass it on to Travis, then received his own. "One was known as the 'Book of Instruction.' The other is called the 'Book of Testimony,' which the prophets talk about." John looked closely at John's face checking to see if he was following this. "Ark of Testimony, you know, the one in the Ark?" Seeing that Travis was paying attention, he continued, "The testimony of the Torah is the books that contained the account of how the Patriarchs kept the Law before Egypt and how they passed it on generation to generation. Because, as you know, the Torah was kept since Eden."

Travis mulled it around in his mind. "Ok. What you are telling me is that the first five books of Moses were written just to remind the Israelites that the patriarchs kept the Torah."

Taking a sip of his now lukewarm cup of coffee, John said, "Yeah, it was the history books of the facts. I have come to understand that the book of Jubilees is a priest's book on the calendar, which I find interesting because of the relationship to the moon. And that is where you come in."

Travis looked puzzled. "What do you mean, where I come in?"

John, working from memory, tried to sum up. "According to the book of Jubilees, 'it' was supposed to appear at a time when Israel was beyond doubting the Torah and started rethinking its traditional position on key issues that make it as a nation stand out; from the rest of the world."

Travis was getting more confused. "What is supposed to appear at the time of doubt?"

John said, "I am not sure."

Travis was now perplexed. "Ok," he said with a half-cocked head and peering at John with one eye closed. "Looks like I will have to read the Book of Jubilees myself someday."

John caught up in what he said, "We will get back to the Jubilees. Later on, let me finish the story I told you earlier that this rabbi told me."

Travis finished his coffee and crumpled up the cup, saying, "Ok?" to encourage John to continue.

John brought his hands together, clasped them, and stretched them out in front until they cracked. Getting his hands back and elbows behind his back in a forward and back motion to take the tightness out from between the shoulder settled in. "The order of Malki-Tzedek is captured by the Jebusites, and they take over Salem. The king of Jebuzites takes over the title 'Adonai-Tzedek,' which was considered blasphemy by those of the Tzedek order. Joshua later defeated the king when the Israelites took over the Promised Land. Thus the school of Tzedek is re-established in Israel. Buuuuuut there is a problem."

"What problem?" Travis asked.

John had Travis's full attention, so he continued. "I don't know if you remember, but when Moses came out of Egypt with the people, God's full intention was that every male was to be a priest. In fact, they were to be a nation of priests. With the order of Tzedek, all males are to be priests, and often it was the eldest who held this position."

"Hey, I am the oldest. Does that mean I would have been chosen?" Travis nudged John in a kidding manner.

"Me too, and in fact, come to think of it, I believe my father is too. We could be of the order of Tzedek," John replied laughingly before continuing, "They continue to exist outside the political and somewhat in the religious arena within Israel even to this day. They have gone so underground that they are almost like a secret society without any known agenda."

Travis remembered. "Hey, aren't you going to tell me the connection King David has to the priesthood?"

John laughed. "So you have been paying attention. When David is anointed to be king of Israel and not too long after comes under the persecution of King Saul, whom does he flee to for support?"

Travis gives him the, 'you got to be kidding me look. "You expect me to remember my Sunday school lessons?"

John sighed, wishing Travis knew more. "In the scriptures, it says that King David met with Zadok, the priest and most people think it is the name of the priest, but what almost every scholar knows is a title of the priesthood. Although at this point in my study, I have some issues that I can't explain. How could the guy named Zadok support the young King David and then serve Solomon for years? The priestly ministry does not start until a man is 30 years of age. I wish more people were taught by rabbis because none of this would have come to light if they had not taken me under their wing and told me this."

They were interrupted by the announcement of turbulence and to fasten their seatbelts. No sooner than the pilot got the words out, the plane took a severe pitch to the right, veering to the left, and tossed like a tumbleweed across the plains on a windy day. Inside, everything was launched, with people who had yet to put their seatbelts on flying through the air and bouncing off the cabin ceiling and walls. Screams resonated in the small space. Panic was setting in as passengers looked wide-eyed with terror.

Travis looked out the window and saw the wall of cloud roll in like the big surf; he had waited so long for one of his favorite Hawaiian beaches. "Surf's Up!" he shouted. "We have an A-frame. Come on, pilot, let's ride it," he called out encouragingly. It was almost as if the pilot could hear him as he maneuvered the plane into a tailwind position. "Ohhh, I am getting amped!" Travis exclaimed as he continued to gaze out the window. "Come on, pilot, this is a good time to do a bottom turn," Travis called out as the pilot steadied the plane. "We can carve ourselves a perfect ride out of this," Travis said to no one in particular, but it was encouraging to the passengers that someone seemed to think it was a rideable situation. Whether he realized it or not, Travis had a captive scared audience, who were now all listening to him narrate as the pilot worked the weather storm raging outside.

"Uuuuhhhhhuup!" John moaned, trying to contain his first inclination.

Looking over at John, who had a sickly green hue about his puffed-out cheeked face, hurriedly grabbed the barf bag for him. "We have caught some sick waves out there, and it is going to be hard trying not to swallow the chowder. Here, take this barf bag, and don't be too clucked out. I think we are going to have some nice firing, and these waves are going to break nicely," he said, trying to reassure John it would soon be over without a major incident. "The pilot is no junkyard dog when it comes to riding this storm out," he said as the plane outran the rolling storm clouds and rose above them with a smooth 180 degrees at the top to get right back on course.

"I see you are a surfing dude," John acknowledged as his color started to return to his face.

"Love it," Travis declared.

And just as soon as it started, it was over. The pilot was very good at quickly righting the plane and getting back on course. People inside the cabin were hurt, some seriously, and those who could help did. Airline flight attendants were quiet and efficient at settling the passengers back into their seats, attending to the injured, and reassuring everyone that everything was under control. The pilot's voice came over the speaker and announced an emergency landing in Adana, Turkey.

John and Travis were stopped by an elderly gentleman as they went to get their stuff out of the overhead, who wanted to thank Travis for the onboard surfer commentary during the plane's rough ride. Some commented on how it helped them remain calm, other remarked that he made it believable that the situation was controllable. Travis blushed and accepted the man's gratitude with graciousness. Others came forward, including the flight attendant, to add their genuine thanks. Travis was overwhelmed and hugged them in thanks. John yanked on his arm and pulled him away from the crowd. "Don't let it go to your head," John grunted as they swiftly moved further down the galley way and out into the terminal.

In the airport terminal, the airport television came on with an English broadcast of 'Airline News.' News of other planes crashing was reported because of the freak storm, which affected the electronics controls on board, and crazy winds in the upper atmosphere, bringing it all home just how serious these solar storms were getting. With the plane's landing, the guys were soon caught up in the final preparations for landing and disembarking. They were fortunate not to be hurt and allowed to leave the airport without too much red tape.

Chapter 13

James returned to Mohaim's home the next evening after a full day of visiting the local library and archives and meeting with the lady that Mohaim had mentioned last night. He found nothing along the lines of what he was looking for. Professor Johan's website pinpointed the exact location of the latest archeological dig. Later that night, he returned for more visiting and fellowship with Ques and family. Sitting down, to a succulent meal, on the pillows scattered on the rugs on the floor with a low-lying table before them, Mahaim started quizzing James about what he knew of the Bacchus. Being a gracious guest, James allows Mahaim the honor of telling the story.

Mahaim beamed as he asked James, "When Antiochus Epiphanes placed the abomination' in the temple, what was it?"

Ques smiled at his brother, knowing where his brother was going with this and looked over to see if James was up for it. James threw out "pig," and Ques chuckled to himself as he looked back at his brother to see how this was all going to play out.

Mahaim said, "If you have read in the book of Maccabees, you will find out that they had set up an abomination of 'desolation' upon the altar. They built altars through the cities of Judea. Jews were made to worship them at their doors, in their homes, and in the streets. But," Mahaim emphasized, "WHICH god did he erect an altar to and make the Jews worship?"

James shugged. "Talmuz"

Mahaim and Ques laughed and gave each other a nod. "It says in 2 Mac 6:7 that it was Bacchus."

James, now puzzled, said, "Never heard of that one."

Mahaim said, "Bacchus is known as Dionisuis," and with that reached over and pulled a book off the shelf and opened up the page to a picture which he handed to James to see. It was a man hung on the cross similar to the one on the Pope's staff. James' mind reeled with the ramifications of this. Mahaim noted that. "This image of Bacchus was found in Palestine."

Ques leaned over to his friend and said, "Now let me tell you a little something." "Yeshua did not die on a cross, and he died on a stake. The Romans used three types of crucifixions: the cross, the X, and the stake. The cross and the X were too heavy to be carried by one man, and they would come in two pieces, not one. Besides that, the Aramaic word "Stake is the actual word used in Latin texts but in Greek only does it get ambiguous."

Mahaim interrupted. "Back to my story here, the Macabees beat Antiochus and restored the temple worship. In fact, the book of Maccabees says that they took over the High Priesthood temporarily until order could be restored. But they don't, they keep it, and the Zadokites are denied the High Priesthood and even partially banned. Later they came to be known as the "doers" of Torah or Assa'im. Maccabees were priests, just not Zadokite priests, and in the generation of Queen Salome, her two sons split on their understanding of faith which, after many years, created two parties, the Pharisees and the Sadducees. The Pharisees were a lay group that opposed the Hasmoneans and claimed to be heirs to an "ancient tradition" which over time came to be known as "oral Torah.".

James, nodding his head, now understood. "So that is how it got popular."

Mahaim leaned forward. "I believe you must find this scroll, for in it lies the truth that has been buried by centuries of lies, and the foundation of our faith has been built on the wrong branch of truth."

James shook his head and raised his hands up in protest. "Hey, I am not interested in disturbing the foundations of any man's faith, and I am only after Hezron's scroll and its whereabouts. For I believe that it would be as great a find as the Dead Sea Scrolls and thus would further my bid for ultimately being the one to have proof of the existence of the Alexandria library or what may remain of it."

The conversation died after that declaration, and the men moved on to lighter subjects that involved what would be the sleeping arrangements and what was next on the agenda.

Chapter 14

After countless hours talking with his contacts in the area and searching for any leads regarding Ques or his brother and ultimately Professor James, Sam finally got an indication that came to bear some fruit. It was in the marketplace where he was questioning merchants, and he eventually ran into someone who gave him the lead he was looking for. Mahalla was a small enough town that one orphan child on the streets pointed out the home of Mahaim for a few coins. Feeling good about knowing where Professor James was again, Sam positioned himself at a local outdoor café within walking distance from Mahaim's home and ordered himself a nice evening dinner.

Lifting a glass to his lips, he turned to see a truck driving erratically down the street towards the local Orthodox Church across the street from the café. Instinctively, Sam ducked behind the café building's pillar just as the blast from the truck went off. Working in Middle East countries for years has honed his instincts well. The church, which should have been appreciated for its historical value, was now wasted in a moment of hatred.

Sam shook the dust off and, picking his way through the rubble, turned to see Mahaim, Ques, and Professor James come out of the house to see what had happened. Not wanting to be seen by the Professor, Sam retreated further inside the café so he could watch them pick their way through the rubble, helping people and checking out how much damage to the building there was. Professor James bee-lined straight into the building and disappeared to the back. Sam thought that was odd and vowed to check into it after the Professor left.

After the Professor had left with his party, Sam quietly moved across the street to explore the church. It was when he got into the very back part of the church that he noticed someone had been cleaning off an area of the floor to reveal a beautiful mosaic pattern which Sam figured was what the Professor came to check on. Quickly took some pictures on his phone and sent them to Karen and the curator, hoping they would go through. He wasn't trusting his phone and called to see if they had received the pics. No answer to either number, and he would have to try again later.

Just as quietly, he left the building to return to his room. It was not in the best part of town, but it did offer him a view of Mahaim's house. The little upper room was plastered and re-plastered in areas but well cared for. In fact, the bed looked as if it had been there since King Tut. Sam pulled up a chair to the window and called to see if he could reach either Karen or the curator. He wondered if Karen received his pics and, if so, had any more information on the mosaic found in the church, what it had to do with the Professor's search, and if the curator was interested in it. But hardly were they connected with they lost their connection.

Chapter 15

Travis and John could not get a flight out because all flights had been grounded for the next few days while the airlines checked on how the weather and solar storms would affect everything. They decided their best chances were to travel by car. It looked like the airlines were no longer safe by any standards, and they were lucky to get as far as they did, given the number of electrical storms and solar flares. In fact, it looked like they were increasing in intensity and frequency. So far, it had not completely knocked out the communication's satellite.

Renting a vehicle was more complicated than they first imagined. All the car rentals were gone, and here they were, stuck in Adana, Turkey, without any available transportation. Heading out the airport door, they decided that the next best thing was to take the local taxi to a nearby hotel while formulating their next plan of action.

Travis brought up the subject of the need to find a vehicle before the computer generation because of its chances of surviving the solar storms and its different effects on sensitive instruments such as a computer.

As they were heading down the road, they saw an old farm truck for sale. It was an American military power wagon that looked like it had been around since the Second World War. The price was right, and the sign said, "Runs Good." At least that is what the driver said. The driver grinned and indicated that he had been listening in on their dilemma and, for a price, was willing to help them. At least, that is what John could figure out from what the taxi driver was saying in broken English. They agreed to have the driver help them negotiate for the vehicle. With a bit of haggling, it wasn't long before the guys were proud owners of a fixed-up antique truck.

The way Travis calculated, the older the vehicle, especially one before the computer age, the better were their chances with easy fixes, and it would not break down from the solar storms. He knew a way around any electromagnetic pulse. Knowing that solar storms would affect the power grid, he had John stop at the local market for supplies; food, flashlights, blankets and a medical kit, and tools to repair the truck engine if it broke down. They got over six gallons of water for the trip and were going to save it for emergency use only. He tried to think of everything he could to be self-sufficient as possible. Just as they were about to leave, John suggested a jerry can full of petrol.

To which Travis said, "What?"

Laughing, John said, "We need a gas can full of gas just in case."

Amused, Travis said, "Ohh yeah, right," and ran back into the market for a suitable gas can. Instead of just one can, he came out of the store with four, "You can never have enough," he said with a shrug. Back on the road, they stop at a gas station, gas up the truck, and fill up the four gas cans.

Travis glanced up into the evening sky as they headed out of town. He is concerned about the solar storms, which he believed would increase in intensity if he had this figured out correctly.

He hoped there would not be any killer solar flares observed on other stars. Some have been estimated to have unleashed enough energy to equal fifty million trillion atomic bombs. Good thing our sun is not as large as Pegasi II, the big red violent star with a binary partner were able to produce, Travis thought. So the worse Travis figured is downed satellite communications and some blackouts here and there on the planet. Travis expected the interference to affect TV, radio, and all digital phones because a lot of the flares were in the short wave radio signals of the high-frequency range.

Solar storms can disrupt communications temporarily but should not, nor is it likely to cause direct harm to the equipment. On the other hand, a massive solar storm could create geomagnetic currents that disable large transformers on the power grid; if this happens, the electric power would be out for years.

What worried Travis was that this could make communications and traveling difficult, and he was starting to wonder if this was such a good idea. The problem was there was no natural easy way of getting back, and besides, he could not leave John to get to his father alone.

So, Travis had John stop on the side of the road to get out a plastic bag and tin foil.

John, with raised eyebrows, watched and asked, "What are you going to do with that?"

Travis smiled as he lifted the hood of the truck. "I am going to protect the truck as best I can from electromagnetic pulses that I believe may come with the next solar storm. I am going to build what I call the nested Faraday cage."

John interrupted, "What!!! What's a nested faraday cage?" he asked, getting out of the truck to look over his shoulder and watch him work.

"What I am going to do is plastic bag the electronics and wrap tin foil over them, so the electromagnetic pulses do not interfere with the truck's electrical system. Now I will not be able to cover it all, but I believe that if we cover the main components and have the truck turned off when the pulse comes, we just might have the only vehicle that works after the storm passes," Travis explained, turning around to face John.

John, shaking his head, said, "Go for it," waving both hands with several flicks, palms down, as if shooing Travis off like a little child wanting to go play.

It didn't take long before Travis had it all in place and secured with electrical tape. It may be a farmer's rigging, but with what was available, it was the best he could come up with, with the supplies they had. He sure hoped it worked as he brushed off his hands on his pants and put the hood down. Soon they were back on the road.

Chapter 16

James was getting a little concerned for his son and his newfound friend. With travel getting more complex and the last he heard from them was well over three days ago, he started to think that maybe having John and Travis come out with his documents wasn't such a good idea. His global cell phone was not picking up any signal, and he knew there was nothing he could do until he heard from them again.

James turned to Mohaim and asked, "Is there a place around here where I can rent a car?"

Mohaim laughed, "There is one place, but I can not guarantee what type of vehicle they will have available. Let me call and see what I can do for you," he said and motioned for James to follow. He took James to a small place where there were two vehicles available. One was a small compact car, and the other was a Jeep. James chose the Jeep. Mohaim was able to negotiate a good deal, and soon they were back at Mohaim's place for the evening.

James sat down with Ques and his brother, opened up the documents he had brought with him along with his notes, and related all he had come to understand about Hezron and his travels. Upon re-reading his notes, a side note caught his attention. It had Qwara circled and a question mark beside it, and nicely written was, "needs more investigation."

So while James had Que's attention, he asked him, "What do you know about Qwara?"

Ques said, "Qwara was in the northwestern part of Egypt beside the Atbara River and was known to be a Jewish settlement as far back as when the Jews were slaves of the Egyptians, according to some sources. Some sources even say that this was the route Moses took on their way upstream from Egypt when they escaped."

James thought about it and agreed. "Since what I figure is the right area, as mentioned in his journal, it could have been the place Hezron visited in his travels."

Ques said, "I do not believe you would find anything there now."

James disagreed. "There is not much there anymore. There might be a home or two that is inhabited now. But we archeologists are all for digging up the past, and it just won't be for this trip. If I need to, I will find funding and authorization to do an archeological dig later."

Ques thought he would throw in this little tidbit of information to round out the conversation. "What you might find interesting is that during Hezron's lifetime, the Talmuds were being written in two different communities, one in Palestine, which is called the Mishna or Palestine Talmud. The other was the Babylonian Talmud which was written about 100 years later. These two have been highly regarded and extensively used for the scattering Jewish community ever since. If Hezron had run into either of these groups, he would have influenced their thinking. Or they would have tried to influence his and what he had written in his journals."

James waved his hands up and acknowledged what was said but interjected with, "My understanding is that Hezron's scrolls were controversial and predating either of these works. Based on that, I would say that those who adhere to either Talmud would find the scroll controversial. I have a suspicion that what is written in the scrolls will have an effect on the religious world as we know it. This could explain some of the commentaries. I have been reading about scholars' thoughts on the subject of Hezron and his scrolls. I do not think that

Hezron was influenced by either. He seemed to be more steadfast in his convictions regarding the scroll and more of a catalyst wherever he went and definitely on those who wrote about him."

"Sorry, but I do not know much more that could be of any help to you," Mohaim admitted.

James, smiling, said, "Thank you for what you do know. I might just be the clues I will need to make some sense of the culture and the religious aspect of what Hezron would encounter."

"You are most welcome," Mohaim said with graciousness.

Lightning flashed, taking out the lights, and the air tingled with sparks as hair stood out from the head. The men all jumped up and ran to look out the window. The view before them was in a blue haze, with static charges giving off sparks, causing the electrical wires to shoot off sparks and the air to smell like an electrical burn. The smoke rising up from different areas was thick enough now to cause the men's eyes to burn. They quickly closed the window, and Mohaim called for his wife to bring them a wash basin. She came in shortly with the towels and basin filled with water. After washing their eyes out, and drying off with the towel, they found that the air had cleared somewhat.

"Have you experienced anything like this?" Ques asked, looking around in the darkened room.

Mohaim shook his head. "Never seen anything like this before. What was it?" he asked as he moved around the room, trying to get the lights to come back on.

James shrugged. "Unless it has something to do with the solar flares, I have not a clue. Do we have any power at all?" he asked. He went over to the window to see how the neighbors were faring.

"It looks like the whole neighborhood has been hit," Mohaim said after surveying the neighbors for lights.

"Listen, I have taken up so much of your hospitality. Time for me to check into my room for the evening. The room is perfect for me, and I appreciate you pointing me in the right direction. I thank you for all you have provided and will be back tomorrow to take a look at this church, you pastor," James said, acknowledging his interest, "Does nine tomorrow morning sound good for you?"

"Yes, that will be fine. Let us pray that nothing worse comes out of these solar flares. May you arrive safely at the room. Do you think that the Jeep will start?" Mohaim asked.

Astonishment came across James' face as it dawned on him that it might not work, so he bolted out the door to check. With a careful check around the Jeep to see if there were any electrical burn smells, he ran his hand along the body to see if it gave off any static charge. It seemed fine. He got into the vehicle and turned on the key, and it fired up just fine. He let out his breath with a sigh of relief. So with a wave at everyone, he headed out to the motel for the night.

Chapter 17

Waking up fully rested after a beautiful evening did wonders for her soul. She stretched like a feline cat, which had just awoken from a nap, and leisurely crawled out of bed to start another day. It was like a short vacation from the work ahead of her, and it made her smile to know that she was appreciated by a fine male specimen of a police officer. Turning on the radio, she listened as it went from the last part of a song into the news report as she started her coffee. The news broadcast reported another satellite had crashed off the coast of England. It went on to say that communications would now be a hit or miss, especially for those who were using global phones or had dish networks.

She would have to wait until Sam contacted her again. She did need to go back to the Professor's house and photograph the maps and charts again. While there, she would check the computer and books she thought might give some indication regarding this case. There had to be something that would indicate what the Professor was looking for, and it could be of interest to the museum.

Karen was getting the impression that the curator was not representing the museum in this matter but may actually be representing a private party. She decided to start her own private investigation into the curator's contacts, especially those interested in Middle East history and archeology in which the Professor was involved. There was some unanswered question running through her mind. Who would be the third party if there was one? Is it the curator or someone else? These were questions that were added to her list of things to investigate.

Driving by the Professor's house, she noticed at least two of the hoodlums who had accosted her standing at the street corner. She idled by and slipped into the alley where she parked further down the alley to not be seen from the street nor have her car identified in association with his home.

Putting on gloves, she found that the door lock had been changed, and easy access was no longer available. She dug through her little bag of tricks and came up with the universal keying system she always used in cases like this. One cool thing about pin-and-tumbler locks is that you can re-configure them to fit an existing key, but in her case, she was going to match the existing lock. Without changing the pattern of the pins, she got an impression that matched the notches. Karen returned to the car and cut a series of notches in a unique key so that it raised each of the upper pins just above the shear line. It didn't take long before she had a key for the lock. In no time, she was back at the door, unlocking it.

Once inside, Karen immediately started taking pictures all on his desk, in the drawers, and in the filing cabinet. All the charts and documents that she had photographed earlier were gone. She moved on to the books on the shelf. But nothing gave her the impression that any of them was significant or essential to this case. All the notes left on his desk had to do with the classes the Professor taught, and the files were on student grading and syllabuses relating to the University classes. She tried to turn on the computer, but there was no power. Then realized that the usual hum of the refrigerator was missing. It must have been one of the reasons that the son was at the house as she looked around, noticing a recently replaced window.

Seeing a dimpled notepad on the coffee table, she took a pencil and rubbed the etchings until they were readable. It looks like someone was making notes, and it wasn't in the Professor's writings. She could not make out what was written. She wondered if one of the young fellows she saw coming out of the building wrote this.

At that moment, she saw a substantial geographic map book with a piece of paper sticking out of the side. Upon opening up the book, she saw it was on the Sinai Peninsula page, and different areas were circled. She made some notes, took photos, and texted them to Sam. She was going to let him figure out if this was valuable info or not.

It was getting late, and after thoroughly casing the joint, she decided that she got all there was left in the building and figured that the boys must have taken the critical stuff she had captured on camera. They must have those documents with them was the only thing she could conclude. She will send what she gathered to the curator and hope that he does not think she was wasting his time with minor details.

Peeking out the door, she saw no one in the alley, and carefully she relocked the door. She turned and was shocked to see a big fellow right in front of her. Just as he made a grab for her, she pushed him with both hands. She made a run for the car. She may have been a good runner, but he was quick at catching up. He had called to his buddy, who came running out of nowhere. She looked back, and one of them recognized her as she recognized him. Now they gave a more serious chase. They must have figured that she was the cause of their latest stint in jail because they looked like they were out for blood this time. Talking about getting even, they soon had her corralled at her car. All her instincts were on the alert and screaming extreme menace. This was getting ugly fast.

"Hey lady, what are you doing back here?" one growled.

Before she could answer, another one asked, pulling out his knife, "Are you helping a friend who had been staying here?" he snarled and menacingly pushed it up against her throat.

"I don't know what you are talking about," she said, trying to sound innocent and lost.

"You know what, lady, I don't believe you," said the ugly one pinning her arms against the car, breathing his putrid breath in her face as he grabbed the keys out of her hand. "If fact, I think that you know too much. So guess what, you are going to come for a little ride with us, where we can discuss this further in privacy." He turned to his accomplice and motioned with his head to shove her into the back seat. He then took her hand and pressed it so high up against her back that her shoulder screamed, and she went up on her tiptoes to ease the pain. With the knife at her throat, he maneuvered her into the car, with himself at her side. His foul-breathed friend ran around and got into the front driver's seat.

Karen looked at the two fellows and then at her situation. The one with the knife at her throat was wiry, cruel around the mouth, like he enjoyed his current power over her. The other one driving was heavy-set, dirty blonde, and his unkempt appearance spoke volumes as his lack of interest in hygiene. She watched warily, looking for an opportunity to get cleanly away.

He was watching her through the rearview mirror, taking in her looks with a perverted interest that was enough to make any woman squirm when unwanted advances touched her in forbidden places. He laughed open-mouthed when he saw what effect he had on her.

She saw the deep cavities, rotting teeth, and the disgusting wad of chew spittle on the corner of his mouth. Her skin shivered in revolt. Peripheral peering at 'old slimeball' next to her. She saw him looking down at her creamy cleavage, and the popped button gave him a clear view. She tried to maneuver her body into a less revealing position. But he was having none of that. With a deepening of the knife into her throat and a sneer on his face, she stopped squirming.

With a turn into an old, seemingly abandoned warehouse, the car disappeared into the darkness of its cavity. The driver quickly got out and slammed the warehouse door down. Moments later, lights came on with a flick of the switch. It revealed a chop shop on the right. Several cars were in various stages of tear down and reconstruction. On the left were filthy remnants of kitchenette cupboards with doors hanging off their hinges, cups, glasses, and dirty dishes littering the counter. Beside the kitchenette was a lounging area strewn with beer cans and bottles in front of a brand new 50-inch LCD TV. Across the back wall was crash bedding scattered across the concrete flooring with an odd assortment of male and female clothing sprinkled haphazardly. She could see a washroom off to the right of the sleeping area. She noticed the door in the far corner on the left side of the big shed doors that she came in on, but no other access that she could tell.

Shoving her out of the car with the knife in her back. The two grabbed her roughly, dragged her to a support post near the lounging area, and tied her down with rope. Once secured, they left her and moved far enough away where she could not precisely hear their conversation, but she figured out it was to discuss what they were going to do next. She could see that without the leader, these two were the grunts of the pack who had never made any further decisions. While they argued, she tried to work the knots out of the rope that held her hands secure as quietly and with the least amount of movements as she could.

Suddenly the old warehouse walls shook off the dust from its shoulders, heaved to its left, and swayed to its right, dropping beams from its rafters and scattering roof shingles like rain as the ground below their feet rumbled and bucked. Both men ran out of the building, leaving Karen to her fate.

Struggling harder and in earnest, she worked frantically to free her wrists from the restraints. Dust rose from the floor as the concrete heaved and cracked as the earth quaked and rumbled. The post she was tied to was now leaning and threatening to fall. Her wrists were bleeding from the frantic struggle as she wiggled to get out of the way of the support post as it slowly started to come out from the floor anchor and slide. The post was out from the ground anchor and hanging freely from the rafters.

Karen scrunched down so that she could bring her hands under the post. Once free, she wiggled her arms down and brought her feet up where she could get her hands in front of her. It was challenging as the ground kept heaving, causing her to fall on her side and bounce.

Coughing from all the accumulating dust, she struggled on, biting on the rope, and finally was able to loosen up the knot where she could unravel it. Parts of the metal wall sheets were coming off the structure as the glass from the windows shattered. It was all falling with the warping and woofing of the warehouse structure to the movement of the ground. The facility was threatening to come down on top of her. She frantically dashed out through a section that had already given way.

With a big whoosh, the structure collapsed, sending a cloud of dust and debris out in all directions. Tossed forward onto a dock, sliding all the way off and into the river, Karen went down amid all the other debris that followed. She surfaced under the dock and stayed there, hanging onto the pier post, waiting until the earthquake was over.

A fire broke out from the combination of broken gas pipelines and electrical sparks. The warehouse next door went up in a fireball explosion as gas drums flew through the air. The water was now on fire from the leakage. With a deep breath, Karen went underwater to swim past the flames towards an opening she noticed on her left. A wave of water carried her out further and faster in a churning, tossing jumble of water and debris as one section of another warehouse collapsed into the water behind her. She was clear of the fire and shore when she surfaced, coughing and sputtering. She swam to a buoy in the bay and hung on exhausted.

Chapter 18

John and Travis saw the devastation of the one insignificant town they were passing through. It had been struck by an earthquake no more than a few hours before they arrived. Buildings were crumbling, staggering, and looked like their sides had been blown away. Streets were heaved, cracked, blocked, and full of debris in spots. It must have been at the earthquake's epicenter with its great crevice tearing the town in two.

Travis jumped out while they were slowly working their way through the traffic to help one woman trying to get her children out from the rubble, and John stopped and followed suit. Soon they had the two children and the mother out of the dwelling. Cuts and bruises were all he could find, as far as Travis could tell, with no serious injuries for any of them.

Through broken English, the mother said, "Thank you," repeatedly. She asked them, "Where are you going?"

She grew very excited when they pointed in the direction they were going. She told them, "My children and I are Christians in a Muslim world!" she gasped, struggling to find the right words. "My husband was killed in the earthquake," she said, pointing to the dead body along the side of the road. "It was the only reason for staying. I no longer have a home, and my family is in the neighboring town. It is not safe for my family or me to be here," she said with tears welling up in her eyes.

Travis looked at John and shrugged, not knowing what to say. John stood there shocked, equally dumbfounded.

She pleaded, with the two little ones now peeping from behind her skirts, with tears continuing to roll down her cheeks. "Please, a ride to my uncle's," she said, pointing to their truck and reaching for Travis's arm, hanging on as if her life depended on it.

She bargained with them. "I have relatives I can stay within the next town." If they were so kind as to take her and her two children, she would be so grateful. "My uncle is in the oil field business, and he often crosses the border to work, which might be a little more difficult for you to cross without his help."

With some inner turmoil, Travis turned to John. "It won't be any trouble to take them to their family, and we are heading that way anyway." Travis convinced John, "It isn't so bad." He added, "She can speak the language, so it might be beneficial as we make our way through Turkey."

John reluctantly agreed. The two children hopped into the front with John, and Travis rode in the back with the mother. The mother only gathered up just a few items that could quickly be found and placed them between her and Travis. She hung on to the side as John jammed the gears, finding second, and with a clutch pop, the truck lurched forward.

They were bouncing down the road when a land mine went off under the vehicle in front of them. The car flew into the air and landed on its side right in front of them. Dust and bodies flying out of it. A fire broke out, and the gas tank blew abruptly, sending pieces of shrapnel everywhere. The explosion caused John's truck to be thrown back from the percussion with parts slamming against the windshield, the passenger door of his truck flipped open, and the little boy went swinging out, riding on the armrest. John threw the little girl out after him, hanging onto the little girl's leg while hollering at her, "Grab your brother." She was able to catch the arm of her brother. John pulled them back in, never slowing down as he went around the tossed vehicle.

He was just about to stop after passing to check on the people in the tossed truck when the children cried out in broken English, "Don't stop! Bad."

Travis hollered from his vantage point, "I don't see anything." Travis kept the woman's head down so that she needed to see the body parts strewn inside the vehicle. Pinging off the rearview mirror, whizzing by his ears, caused John to dodge, and as he ducked, he pushed the children down onto the floorboard. John put the pedal to the metal and hurried out of town. He was not going to stop because he wasn't too sure if there would be any more factions ready to shoot any and all vehicles.

Travis and the woman in the back dropped quickly into the truck's bed and hung on. John wasn't going to take any chances. Travis saw a group of armed men come out of a building to the right as they passed. They were far enough away, but Travis encouraged, "Move it, move it,"

Liking the idea of getting as much distance between them and the armed men as quickly as possible. The rest of the trip was given to thoughtful and stoic persistence. As they all quietly moved on down the road. Once out of the town and its wreckages, it was an uneventful ride to the woman's hometown. She pointed out the house and, when the truck stopped, ran around to the front passenger side to gather her children about her.

Travis jumped out of the back seat and moved into the vacant spot on the passenger side. John was about to head out when she motioned them to come inside and meet her family. Travis and John protested in unison, "It is not necessary."

She would not be dissuaded, and she told the children to go get her uncle quick. They ran inside as she grabbed John's arm, pleading with him to stay. Family members poured out of the home. Three prominent men, several women, and four or five children have soon gathered around. She explained to her family, "These men rescued her and her children, and now they needed help." She turned to Travis and John, "Please let us help you as you have helped us. You do not know how difficult it is to cross the border and your best chances are with my uncle."

The men came forward and gave them hugs of gratitude for rescuing her and more than encouraged them to go inside and eat. Introductions were made, with her doing most of the interpreting. Her uncle knew the odd word here and there and tried to make conversation. But it seemed like he was making more of an effort to learn more English words from them.

Travis and John found themselves in a small dwelling sitting on the carpet before a massive wok-style plate of food and encouraged to eat, drink, and eat some more while the children shyly looked on. The rest of the evening, they talked with her interpreting. They were hearing about the local news and learning about what to expect on the road ahead. The uncle, eager to pick up more words of English, continued to repeat them as she spoke them, and they helped with the correct pronunciation once they figured out what he was trying to say. Travis and John, in turn, tried to pick up the Turkish language, and many laughs were had by all at the fumbling attempts by both parties.

The woman's uncle was in the oil field as a perforating engineer, where he was to go out to drilling sites and take seismographic readings. The company he worked for covered most of the Arabic states. If they wanted to, since he was heading down to the Qala'at Samaan, which was across the border into Syria tomorrow, they could travel with him. He suggested that the chances were better by traveling with him as if part of his company. They would be able to get across as American drilling engineer consultants rather than tourists. John and Travis thought he might be right and agreed to travel with his company the following day.

Given a spot on the floor that night, they rested until morning. The uncle woke them up at dawn the following day, and quietly they left without disturbing the scattered sleeping bodies lying all over the floor. Some sleepy heads did wake up and bid farewell to their newfound friends, the group heading out for the border.

They arrived at the border by noon. With a bit of money passing hands and friendly conversation from their uncle with the border patrol, they could cross over easily. He seemed to know the border patrol well.

When they came to a fork in the road, he pointed them in the southerly direction and told them that he would be heading up to the rig site. With that, the boys found themselves running across some barren, dusty road towards Lebanon.

Travis looked at the map. "What do you think of the idea of picking up a plane and flying since it looks like there looks like a lull in sunspot activity right now."

John looked at the cell phone service to see if he had any reception, "My cell phone is back up, but I have not been able to get through to my father. It goes dead when I think I have a strong enough signal. You know better than me about the solar storm activity, and do you really think it is finally over?"

"No, not really. I am tired of a hot, dusty road in an old truck that seems to be able to accentuate every bump in the road. I do not know how people put up with this kind of slow transportation in the old days. But it is just killing me, and I consider myself fit," Travis said, shifting in his seat for a more comfortable position.

"After seeing the solar storms can do, I will take my chances on the ground riding in this old beast. Thank you very much," he said, patting the dashboard with affection before turning towards town. "See, here we are up on this high ridge, and hey, I have a signal," he said, trying again to connect with his father.

John said, "Hey, dad. Dad, can you hear me?" slowing the truck down to the side of the road, shutting the engine so that he could hear. "We have a truck and are driving, and we should be in Jerusalem sometime next week if all goes well. How soon will you be there? "John listened intently to his father. "How about we meet at our favorite location like last time? If you or I get there first, leave a note under a rock by the monument." Nodding his head and with a couple of "Yeah, yeah" here and there as he listened until the phone died. John then turned to Travis and said, "Right now, my father indicated that he was heading to the archeological dig site his friend was on. We should arrive in Jerusalem about the same time if all goes well."

Following along the Bishri Mountains that dominated the flat desert, the boys silently watched the landscape pass. It was hot, dry, and with a temperature above 105. They kept their heads inside the cab, the windows open so that the breeze, shirts wide open to catch the cooling effect, which gave them some relief, and they drank their water in small sips. Just enough to keep their lips moist.

As the road meandered closer along the Mediterranean coastal areas, there was an afternoon rainfall that was quite nice and, with it, brought the temperature down to a pleasant level. The humidity did stay relatively high, and the boys were soon drenched in their T-shirts. So the boys went from high and dry to coastal wet by an evening at Taurus.

John suggested as he spotted a town, "How does crashing at this town tonight sound to you?" Just as they crested the top of the hill overlooking the valley, the fiery ball streaked across the sky really low on the horizon across the Mediterranean waters and, like lightning, headed towards the earth in one zigzag line of fire, torching the town below as it splashed down on the earth.

John came to a screeching halt in shock as they opened, mouthed watch the scene transpiring before them. In rapid fire, the streaks pelted the valley, lighting up the whole area like a war zone. But this was no military fire they had ever witnessed on TV, and this was a devastating effect of the solar flare touching the earth.

The flare fires were quickly pelting close and closer, heading their way. John backed up. He hastily turned the truck around. Gunning the motor, he headed back the way they came. A couple of really close calls as the flares zinged the earth behind them. They could feel the charge in the air and could feel the heat.

Travis hollered, "Faster, faster," as he hung on to the dashboard in a death grip. All went quiet. Travis, checking the sky turned to John and said, "It looks like it is over." John slowed down to a stop. They turned on the radio, and Travis searched for an English radio station.

In between the crackling and buzz, they could detect an English broadcast, which Travis stopped at. "...And now for our special report. Over forty places were hit, covering an area so large that it splattered the upper region of the Mediterranean from Rome to Turkey... static... It went as far north as Serbia. The worst hit was Sofia in Bulgaria, where the firestorm rained over a 100-mile area, killing untold numbers.... static... What was determined is that a planet X had been attracting the sun's molten flow like the moon draws the waves of our sea. Since the planet was on the other side of the sun and not seen, ..static... Dr. Pagett of the Colgate University in Hamilton, New York, postulated that it was held prisoner of the sun's gravity pull and when slingshot ... static... from behind the sun, the sun's molten wave ...static.. followed in one substantial solar flare that reached out and touched the earth. The winds that had been affecting the earth ... static.... Earlier were from solar activity. Planet X will not be returning for another 2000 years. ...static... We will keep you posted on the details of the damage static.. as they come in. Because of the damage, communication is down in many areas. It will ... static... before we can determine how bad the situation really is. Most government bodies are busy working... static... on getting the infrastructure up and have evoked ... static.. martial law. ... static.. riots in the street, several areas have been taken over ... static.. various factions....static...looting, fires .. Static.. are breaking out all over the place. And that is the latest news in this special report. We will keep you posted on any new developments. And now back to your regularly scheduled program." Music once again filled the airwaves.

Travis turned to John and said, "We need to get out of here. I hope there is another town not far from here and that it is safer than where we are now. I don't think we will be seeing anything like that again."

"We need to go down to that village and see if we can help," John said, turning the truck around and accelerating back the way they had just from.

"No, we need to keep moving," Travis retorted, anxiously looking up at the sky.

"No, I am heading down there to see if I can help," John said with determination as he manhandled the manual steering on the truck into as tight a turn as it possible could go. The truck refused and squealed in protest.

Travis more strongly declared, "Don't!" reaching across to grab the wheel to keep John from making the turn.

John pushed Travis' hands off the wheel and, in doing so, jerked the truck off the road. The old clunker died in the ditch with a 'kerchunk' against the embankment. Shifting gears into reverse, John gunned it. The rear wheels only spin, sending dirt flying on the undercarriage as it dug itself in deeper. Switching from reverse to forward, John rocked the truck to gain traction, but it only dug in more profoundly into the sand. John pissed off, hits the steering wheel, and glares at Travis. "Now, look what you have done!"

"I have done?" retorted Travis. "Do you have any idea what you are doing?" he asked, swinging his body around to point down at the village, which John took advantage of to shove Travis out of the vehicle. Travis tumbled out of the truck and hit the sand with both knees. Getting up angrily, he reached across and grabbed John, hauling him bodily out of the vehicle and onto the sand. John kicked Travis with both feet across the vehicle's hood and hopped up. Travis took advantage of his momentum and pulled him forward onto the ground in one swift pull. Travis turned to the truck. John retaliated with a grab at Travis' feet as he head off to push the truck out of the embankment, causing him to tumble forward.

Now both are in earnest. Fists flying, jabs to the ribs, a volley of painful grunts when contacts were made, and each struggling to be the victor. Finally, Travis had John pinned down by sitting on him with his knees pinning down John's arms.

Several more attempts at a struggle to extract himself from his current position made John realize that Travis wasn't letting up. His body went limp as the struggle and anger left his body. He cried out, "Why not, don't you care about them?" through an outburst and exasperation.

Travis easing up on his hold, looked down at John and quietly answered, "Listen. Listen real closely. Do you hear anything coming from the village? We are not that far. We should hear some faint cries, moans, or painful screams, and we don't. Other than the sounds of embers burning, can you hear anything? Because I hear no voices, no cries, or other sounds of life." And for emphasis, he shouted, "Nothing!" throwing his arms up to encompass the whole area.

John listened really hard. Not moving, hoping to hear something that would indicate that someone was alive and needed help.

Travis, seeing that John had calmed down, got off of him. He ambled off to the front of the truck, where he checked to see how deeply embedded into the embankment it was.

On the other hand, John climbed up the embankment, looking down into the valley at the village to see if he could make out any life moving about. Running back to the truck's bed, he pulled binoculars out of his bag and ran back up the embankment to scan the area for life.

Travis meandered over after giving John time to do a thorough search. "With the intensity of sun firestorm, the chances of life were remote at best. We were lucky to be as far out of range as we were."

Slowly John turned to Travis and apologized for shoving him out of the truck, "Sorry, but I really thought you were being a self-centered ass who didn't care about human suffering."

"I hope not." Travis raised eyebrows and stepped back to take another look at John, as if not being able to believe someone would believe he was even remotely like that. "We need to get the truck unstuck and get back on the road," Travis reminded John.

Wrapping the strap of the binoculars around his neck, John joined Travis in shoving the truck back out of the embankment. John hopped back into the truck, threw it into reverse, and got it back on the road with Travis's help pushing it from the front fender.

Once they were back on the road again, heading towards their destination, John grimly looked in the rearview mirror at the devastation and futilely asked, "Do you think that maybe we should go back and just see if we can be of any help?"

Travis emphatically said, "No!" and crossed his arms in resolute determination. He had a dreadful feeling that everything was charred beyond recognition. Something he did not want to see. "There is more where that came from, and we are in the belt line of the sun's travels. I am not interested in being a crispy critter! He said with a crinkled nose.

John shuttered and nervously chucked at the visual. Travis joined in.

Chapter 19

Sam emailed Karen from the internet café' what he had, checked all the information she had gathered, and emailed it to him. It was prolonged Internet service and took up most of the afternoon before they could send each other the most current information. It had to be resent and resent, along with the computer having to be rebooted numerous times. Frustration was mounting for Sam as he almost spilled his coffee on the keyboard. He quickly wiped the spots off the keys with his napkin, looking around to see if the owner saw it.

Patience was not Sam's strong point, and he was having a tough time with the computer slowness. Slipping over to another table, he could get into his email. Finally, he successfully received and sent all the information on the case he had gathered so far.

Sitting at the outdoor café table, with his coffee before him, he dug out all the papers he printed from the computer transmissions. The map of the Sinai Peninsula with several locations marked out might just be the clues he is looking for as to where the Professor was heading. He had run out of options and decided that his next best bet was to head towards one of the marked places and snoop around. There was one place in particular on the map with Hezron beside it. He figured that he could go there and gather up any information on this Hezron while he puts out feelers. Satisfied that this was the best route to take, he gathered up all his material and was just about to go to the nearest lodging place for a place to stay the night. *Tomorrow would be another day*, were his thoughts as he looked for change to give as a tip before rising.

Across the table from where he was sitting was the mob that had busted into Ques' house. They looked suspiciously at him and were talking among themselves, making Sam uneasy. One of them got up from his table and started heading in his direction, with a couple behind him to back him up. They were making quick work of the three tables between them.

Just as they reached his table, the sky went a static gray that sizzled and crackled like a massive amount of static. Sparking off all metal and electrical devices, a few exploding caused a panic in the streets as cars caught fire, and cell phones popped, even Sam's. The computers cracked and sent up smoke signals with their dying breath. Startled, the mob members were caught up in the ruckus, trying to get cell phones and other electronic devices out of their pockets. Sam took this as a good time to disappear. He quietly left the area while all others were gazing around them at the chaos.

Without his cell phone, Sam was on his own. He was without communication in a foreign land. Without any idea where the Professor really was, Sam was worried. Now without any chances of getting a hold of Karen gave him an uneasy feeling. Stranded on assignment was not new to him, but with the strange goings on in the air and weather, it did make him nervous. Being in a foreign country where he had no connections or contacts to turn to, and was not fluent in the local language, didn't help either. Besides, he thought, as he looked around, these people were getting edgy like they were acting like anyone, not of their faith, was at fault, as he saw suspicious eyes turn his way.

Sam decided that he needed to go to the local market and buy a few items, like the prayer rug and a turban, to help blend in. Scooting through the narrow alley, he made his way to the marketplace, where he earned his purchases. Business in the market was closing up rather quickly as everyone was gathering their wares and securing them hastily.

Sam was fortunate to find a merchant still in the process of closing with just the items he needed. He pleaded his case, finger pointing and flashing money. His wild pleading gestures of the need to pray helped get the merchant to relent and sell Sam the necessary items. It must be the strange static in the air that was causing them to close up shops. Now with his prayer shawl and turban neatly tucked around his head, he felt that blending in would be easier. He didn't want to stand out as much as he headed off out of the marketplace.

He started back in the direction of his hotel and hoped his car would start up. He might have to return it to the rental company at the airport and get another one that works. That is, if there was one. Looking around him at what vehicles were moving down the road, he noticed very few vehicles traveling on the road. Looking closer, it dawned on Sam that all pre-computer chip models were the only ones moving. So much for the idea that a rental car would work, as they would all be new models. It looks like he was going to have to do some wheeling and dealing for an old beast.

As he wandered the streets, he came across an old farmer who had come in with his produce in a beat-up old truck, and it was idling. He went up and with mimes and a few words here and there, and he was able to interest the farmer is selling. It was an old International, a former Coca-Cola delivery truck. There was rust out along the lower edge of each door. It was an extremely rare truck that was nearly complete. From what Sam could see, the engine and trans were there, but it will need to be rebuilt eventually. It even had the original Coke bed. The old farmer hated to get rid of it, but he was desperate for the money.

The truck looked like it came from the Second World War. It was battered, faded, and rusted out. The farmer was a hard bargainer, and Sam felt taken when the deal was struck. But then again, it seemed to be running fine. Glad to have it in any condition, Sam quickly paid the man and headed back to the hotel to pick up his stuff and head out. He had enough of this town.

Chapter 20

James left Ques with his family and rented another vehicle to head down to Atbarah, Sudan, where Professor Johan Goldberg was digging. He was able to contact the Professor and understood that it would take a few days to travel to get down there, and since his son and friend were going to take a while to get to Jerusalem by car, he was free to make this side trip before heading north.

The journey was uneventful, and the weather was nice. James made good time down the road, enjoying the vistas and ethnic foods and flavors as he went. It took a little bit to find a boat to take him across to the island just north of Atbarah, where the Professor's site dig was.

Professor welcomed his old friend. "Good to see you," he said, taking the protruding hand of his friend.

"You are looking well. I see you have lots of help," James said, looking over at the nine other people working at various tasks around the camp.

"I know exactly why you have come," he said, motioning James to come over to the big tent situated on the north side of camp.

"Really, now what do you have that you believe could of even remote interest to me?" James asked, nudging his friend with a smile on his face.

"If that is what it takes for you to come, then the least I can do is show you the find that I believe you will find most interesting," he said.

Taking him immediately over to the table of broken pottery, a stone tablet with a circle within a circle and symbols all around the inner ring and outer circle. While they could make out some of the characters of constellations, there were some unfamiliar symbols not seen before. Professor James Holden was given the privilege of taking photos of the stone.

This stone looked like some timetable of the stars in relation to the seasons. Each of the twelve pronged stars whose nucleus was in the center pointed to a specific astrological sign. Symbols of a woman, balances, scorpion, archer, goat, water fish, ram, bull, twins, crab, and the lion made up the twelve signs. Between the fish and the water was the small circle that seemed to break up the cycle. It was indeed a puzzle as to what the small circle in the ring meant.

Johan, pointing to the different symbols, remarked, "Did you know that in the bible it is called the mazzaroth and it is the Greeks that named it the zodiac which in both languages mean "the way" or "the path" but has two entirely different contexts. To the Greek mind, it is a personal map of one's life depending on which star you were born under. To the Hebrew people, it was the story of redemption that God put in the sky for signs and seasons. So horoscopes and astrology are vastly different from how sages saw it."

James asked, "How so?"

"The sages see, for example, Virgo as the one who brings forth and Libra with the balances with judgment. Each period would only last while each constellation was in the "house" which could last for years, and afterward, that "house" prophecy would be over."

Turning to face Johan and giving him a blank stare, James said, "You lost me."

Rubbing his forehead and thinking about how he could rephrase this so that James could understand, Johan paused and thought long and hard about how he could answer. Then looking up into the night air, he bodily turned in a circular motion and pointed out sets of stars and gave them names, showing their positions as he circled around

James. "Ok, the scorpion and archer are together. It is because of the battle between good and evil since the Garden of Eden. The archer has his bow drawn and aimed at the scorpion while the scorpion is at the heel of the archer, symbolizing how it all will fulfill the promise of God at the Garden of Eden when Adam and Eve got kicked out."

Johan was about to continue when James interrupted him. "You know, come to think of it, many famous people are known for their achievements, like the Bishop who reformed the calendar or Johann Kepler who discovered the fundamental laws on which the solar system is built. Even the calculation of the meridian running through Greenwich was based on the Zodiac sign, Aries. Which is where we get our time from?"

Glad to see James catching a glimpse of the effect star gazers had on what we know today. "Yes, it affects many different sciences and basic understandings. We use many things today as standards based on calculations of various star gazers throughout the centuries. Here is something interesting. Capricorn," he said once again, pointing out a constellation. "This animal is part goat and part fish. The goat is the one that really comes into focus during the Yom Kippur ceremonies in the biblical feasts because it is the sacrifice to cleanse and separate the congregations from their sins. My problem is that I haven't yet put the story together with events. At least, not like the ancients believe," Johan expounded.

Going back to the etchings and comparing the stars' constellations with the etchings, James could now relate the stars and their images together. "This is fascinating, a study that I have not really given much thought to. I think you might be on to the Jewish fascination that Hezron and those who followed him had with stars and what the signs of heaven mean."

"Well, then let me tell you more." Johan once again points up to the sky. "Then comes the water bearer, which we know as Aquarius, pouring out the endless supply of water where Pisces, the fish, dwells. As you know, fish cannot survive without water. By the way, each sign represented one of the twelve tribes of Israel and their time to shine forth."

"So where are we, in the constellation, as far as which 'house'?" James asked.

"We are about to enter the age of Aquarius according to the Mayan Calendar."

Johan then goes on to elaborate, but James interrupted with, "So why is the circle within the winged circle between Pisces and Aquarius?"

Johan stared intently at the etchings before him with a frown on his face, rubbing his whiskers, and then said, "I think we need to be looking at this as a constellation, with each tine of the star, whose nucleus resides in the center, pointing to a circular window. I have not yet seen it on any of the other ancient constellation maps, have you?"

James laughed. "No! But ok, which is true science and simply a concoction of mumbo-jumbo? Are they symbols of the ancients using stars to tell stories and trying to make sense of their universe, or are they constellations mapped out in conjunction with natural pathways?"

Johan smiled and rested his hand on James' back while pointing to the symbols. "While I can say for sure which way they understood or what they are trying to say. Here, it is not beyond the possibility those earlier astrologists complied with their skills and were able to make the movements over the centuries as they passed on the understanding from generation to generation. Since various forms of stargazers used the stars for various mappings out of the patterns of the sky to project their understanding of the future, I would say this is just one man's or one tribe's understanding," he said. And with that, Johan offers something to eat by pointing to his refrigerator and changing the subject with, "It is getting late."

With the thought of food, James' stomach started to loudly rumble, and they both laughingly turned toward Johan's tent. James was not willing to give up the subject. "Back to the subject of the circle within a circle between Pisces and Aquarius, you said that we are approaching the end of Pisces, the fish, and I thought about Jesus and his fishers of men. You can tell I have been to see Ques before stopping in to see you, but is that a coincidence or what?"

Johan, a man of faith, nodded. "It was the symbol of their faith, so I am sure that Venus playing the Bright Morning Star position does help strengthen the idea. I bring this up because it is a title that Jesus is given in Revelation 22, which refers to him as the Alpha and Omega. In 2001, there was a rare astronomical event. Venus loped around the alpha star of the constellation instead of moving through a constellation, and it ended up at the omega star of the same constellation. I have always wondered if there is a relationship with the sign of the Son of man in heaven."

James shrugs and blows off any religious connotations with a "Doubt it. How about the circle within the circle with wings? Is it nothing more than a face of one of the ancient gods?"

"To the best of my knowledge, that has never been represented like this in any other ancient constellation chart," Johan said, shaking his head.

"True, true," he said, looking more closely at it to see if there was anything else about it that might give a clue as to its meaning.

Johan shook his head and said, "Position dictates that it is something else. I have no answers as of yet as to why the circle within a circle with wings, though." and with that, dropped the subject.

"I will be meeting with my son and his friend. He is an astrophysicist, so you can be sure I will be asking him. Maybe he can clear this up for us. May I make an etching of it?" James said, seeing that they both may have reached the limit of their knowledge for now.

"I have already made a copy for your files because I knew that you would want to study it further," Johan said as he turned to his makeshift desk.

Chapter 21

Travis and John quickly backed up and headed in a westerly direction hoping to go around the smoldering and fire-razed valley. They were sickened and saddened by the devastation below but knew there was little they could do not knowing the language, not knowing the area, and not knowing if their help would be appreciated. John offered up a silent prayer.

Travis checked the map to see what alternative route they could take when John grew silent and reflective. The silence between them was punctuated by Travis' directions as John continued to drive. There was no other traffic for the rest of the trip, and John's phone service was no longer working.

It grew dark, and with no town in sight, they decided to pull off on the side of the road where they saw a few trees up against a hillside. Getting into the back of the truck, they settled in for the night. The backpacks worked as pillows, and the extra clothing they put on worked to take some of the chills out of the evening air. They built no fire so as not to attract any unwanted attention.

Later that night, after John had drifted off to sleep, Travis felt the need for relief from a full bladder and got up to find a spot to relieve himself. It was a beautiful moonlight night, and the crickets and other night animals gave the world a sense of peace. The stars were out in a gorgeous array, seemingly more of them than what he had seen with his naked eyes back in the States. But that was to be expected. Here no city or town lights interfered with the view. No smog to cloud the sky.

Travis got caught up in his love for the actual night lights nature offered that truly enchanted him since he was a child. With eyes gazing up more than down, he took in the vastness of the universe, the beauty, and fascination with its multi-facet organization and parade across the skies.

Climbing around the boulder, Travis tripped and fell face first onto the ground, which gave way and sent him sliding down into a hole. With sand pouring in after him, Travis was soon trapped. When the dust settled, Travis looked up to see how far down he was, and it didn't look too far. Trying to get out from under the sand was going to be extremely difficult since his left arm was trapped under his body. From his waist down, he was buried in the sand. He wiggled his toes and fingers and didn't feel anything broken.

Calling out several times, Travis hoped that John would wake and hear him. His voice echoed silently in the chamber. This didn't sound good. He focused on trying to get his left arm out. Maybe he could free his left arm and dig himself out. Wiggling his fingers, he was able to create some wrist room, and by shifting his shoulder, he moved his arm up. His body was acting like a barrier to the shifting sand. He dug under his rib cage upwards towards the top of his sternum. It was inch by inch, slow progress. Every once in a while, he would rest and call out. He listened, but the air was still; not even crickets were making a sound. On through the night, he worked on freeing his hand. Resting, working, and calling out, he had his hand free by sunrise and was now able to work on getting some of the sand off his back. But no matter how hard he tried to pull himself out, he was unable to move much.

Then he heard John calling out for him, and he hollered back. It was not too long before John found the hole and could see Travis at the bottom.

"Are you hurt?" he asked, getting on his knees. John peered in.

Waving at John, Travis tried to get John's attention as to where he was trapped, "No. I am over here."

"Can you get yourself out?" John asked, now spotting Travis way down to the left side of the cave-in.

"Been working on that all night, not having much luck," Travis said, pointing to his waist where the sand held him down.

John told Travis, "I am going back for the chain behind the seat." John ran back to the truck and grabbed the chain. He ran back and threw one end down the pit, but it was not long enough. John hollered down that he had an idea and was gone again. Travis could hear the truck start up, and soon it sounded really close. John was quickly back at the pit entrance. "I have tied off the chain to the truck's bumper and will climb down and help dig you out. We will be able to pull ourselves back up from there."

Soon John was down there helping Travis dig his way out. The sun was rising and flooded the room with light. Once Travis was out of the sand, they sat, catching their breath and looking around the pit.

"Hey, look over there. Do you see it?" John asked, pointing to something sticking out of the sand.

"See what?" Turning in the direction that John was headed towards.

"I don't know. It looks like something leather. Here let me go see." Travis was up and now not far behind him.

Digging in the sand, John soon had a leather satchel and brought it back to where Travis was sitting. Together they opened it up to see what was in it. Inside was a parchment scroll which they were cautious with. The parchment seemed to be old and fragile. Nothing else seemed to be in the satchel, so they returned the parchment.

"I bet my dad can read this. We will have to remember where we found this and tell my dad. But in the meantime, I think it is high time to get out of this pit. Are you up for it?" John said as he dusted off the satchel.

"Yeah, I think I am ready. I will go first so that you can push me up if necessary. I am worn out from trying to dig myself out last night and do not know how much strength I have left," Travis said as he grabbed onto the chain and began working his way to the top.

"No problem," John said, looking into the satchel again with growing excitement at just what they might have run across. The pit was not giving him proper lighting to see much, so he made minimal effort to look further.

Without too much trouble, they could get out of the pit and back on the road. Being hungry and tired and ready to see some civilization, they were delighted to see a village over the next ridge. Laughing in disbelief, they shook their heads at the that they spent the night one ridge over from civilization roughing it.

Pulling up to the first café they could find, they were soon served coffee so strong the spoon stood up on its own, along with a hot dish with fruit and bread. Travis looked at all that was before them with appreciation and said, "Get in my belly," pointing to his stomach before lifting up the fork.

It was as if they were starving; they dug right in without much ado and lots of gusto, other than John saying a brief, heartfelt quick thankful prayer to the Lord. Asking for seconds, they continued to eat and drink without much talk. They hardly looked up from their plates and polished off the food in rapid order. Finally, John leaning back, patting his gut, sighed. Travis looked around at their surroundings and noticed all the locals watching them with intense interest. In fact, they were encircled. Travis smiled and looked around towards the server, to whom he gave the thumbs up sign, and said, "That was wonderful. Thank you."

John, picking up on the icy surroundings permeating the crowd that had gathered, quickly realized Travis was trying to defuse a potentially dangerous corner they had inadvertently walked into. He started to rise, and the group moved in menacingly closer. Smiling real friendly-like sat back down. He searched the crowd for a leader to whom he could offer his hand of friendship. Spotting one of the men, whom they seemed to be getting their eye signals, he approached him. He was immediately blocked by a wall of humanity from advancing any further.

Travis had moved to John's back with his back against John's in a protective stance. Travis estimated about eight men. Most of them were young, with a couple older ones towards the back. He kept smiling, nodding his head at each of the men before him. Looking for some type of compassion in any of the faces. He took in the distance to their vehicle. The other patrons of the café just watched. There was an absence of any help coming from any other quarters. And the fact they were the only foreigners. The air tingled with tension.

Again rumbling started coming up from the earth, and the sound increased as the ground began to shift and shake. Tables and chairs moved across the sidewalk, and people grabbed anything close to them to keep from falling. The rumbling grew into a roar. Travis and John, like everyone else, were tossed to the ground, thrown around, and mixed in with the churning of the earth. The café crumbled, and the road opened up as Travis and John started crawling away.

It was a madhouse of screams and cries as everyone was scrambling in every way they could to escape. Flames leaped upward from a broken line underground through a crack under the sidewalk. The street humped into a ridge, and a part of the sidewalk on the other side sunk, taking the building with it.

The truck was heaving up on the ridge when Travis reached it. Telephone poles were swayed, leaning over and whipping back in a rhythm like that of an unseen conductor's wand during his frantic piece of operatic crescendo as the earthquake grew in magnitude. A great water main burst forth in the middle of the street, no more than a block from where they were. John was right behind Travis, trying to keep from sliding down the ridge when it all stopped just as suddenly as it started.

The boys lost no time in getting into the truck, taking off, spitting rocks, and bouncing out of town before the locals could get their wits about them and see that they had left. One stood in the middle of the street, throwing rocks at their disappearing vehicle. John kept looking back as Travis navigated the truck in and around the bad spots in the road. In some places, large boulders from the parts of the building crumbled onto the street and blocked their way. Working around the cracks and depressions in the road, around the crumbling ground and rubble, avoiding the scrambling crowds in the streets, they drove out into the countryside before they slowed down. John checked to make sure they still had the satchel. Travis kept his eyes on the road wanting to get as much distance as possible, just in case someone decided to follow them.

As John looked in the satchel, his mind flashed back to the skeleton holding this satchel and wondered who he was.

Chapter 22

Hezron was now free. He was so profoundly thankful that he just couldn't stop thanking the Lord for the merchant who set him free. Setting course for Jerusalem, Hezron traveled with the merchant to the next village, where they parted company. It was there that Hezron met with the chief priest and his council. He thought what he might do was hand the scroll over and be free of the burden placed upon his heart. He had prayed he had found the right person in the local chief priest to give the scroll to.

Ben Moshech, the chief priest, and his council gathered to read over the parchment that Hezron had given them. Prophesied in the parchment were the coming days with wickedness overflowing and a call to repentance on Rosh Hashanah, destruction of the homes, and the need to flee to the mountains when the moon eclipse was on the first high holy day of the Feast of Sukkoth.

Based on the calculations of the moon cycle as taught in the parchment, this year was the year that the feast would have a moon eclipse. It talked about the days of Niribu, which came from Orion, causing upheavals of earth, oceans, volcanoes, and weather during this time period. In the parchment, God declares that when all these things come to pass, know that He will go forth to save his people. There was much discussion of the prophecy and its accuracy. What to do about it? Which kept the priest and his council busy for days.

They quizzed Hezron, whose name means trouble, on how he came across the other parchment and listened to him relate the story of the fellow traveler and how he came to be in possession of it when the library caught fire. As a librarian, he had never believed it should have been taken to the library. It was not well known that the library had it in its possession, so when the fire broke out during a schism between religious factions and the political-military-driven faction, Hezron took the opportunity to rescue this scroll. They continued to ask him more and more questions, and the more they asked, the more agitated they became. It didn't seem to be directed at him. But instead, at his story of how he came to be the carrier of the scroll. Hezron was getting more curious as to why.

Hezron told them of the time when the children of Moses lived beyond a river of grinding, which was impossible to visit except on Shabbat when the river ceased to grind. He said that before his capture as a slave, he visited this tribe of rabbis and warriors who were ruled by a king assisted by a learned Torah judge prophet, Flash. It was at his feet he did learn the understandings what was written on the parchment. Flash was of the Melchizedek order and understood the constellations and the story of redemption they told from the winged ones.

Later that night, after settling for a night's rest, Hezron was surprised by a visitor when all was quiet. One of the elders came to talk with him more about his traveling companion and how much of the parchment he read and understood. They talked long into the night about how this fellow companion was retelling a story of a family member long ago who felt compelled to take the parchment from their village so that what was prophesied within would not happen to them. Now that the parchment had returned to its home, they were sure it was to come to pass. The priest had petitioned Hezron to leave the scroll with them. The priest declared that he was given a dream about the scroll's return and leaving it with them.

Hezron explained that he had many years to study and understand what was written in that parchment and seen how everywhere he had traveled over the years, the prophecies contained within were benefiting the city and its people at the time he was residing in it. Each time it required repentance of the city and its people, the wickedness would sweep over their lives and destroy their world, and they would have to flee to the wilderness until they repented of their deeds. This they promised to do.

The priest continued to present to Hezron the importance of leaving the scroll with him. So persuasive was the priest that Hezron promised to leave the parchment with them, which he documented in his travel journal later that night before bedding down for the night. To not lose it again, the elder announced, "It would be written in stone to stand the test of time."

Hezron thought it was an excellent idea. He promised to stay and help them with this task. That night he had a dream. He dreamt that all that was given to him was taken away, and he felt in his heart that God was telling him to not leave this parchment with these people. He woke up with a start and realized that he could not give the parchment to them but leave them a copy of his journal. He could, as God had chosen someone else, receive the original, even if it originated in this village as the priest proclaimed.

Hezron decided it was high time for him to return to Jerusalem and return the documents to the rightful owners. He made his announcement to those he had been staying with. He bid shalom to the priest and the farewell gathering, handing over the copy he had made of the parts of the parchment they were most interested in. With his meager belongings, gifts from friends, and a horse for the journey, he headed out. It wasn't long before he joined up with a caravan running in the same direction, which brought him comfort, knowing that it was safer to travel in numbers.

At night he would look up at the stars and retell the story as it was played out in the stars to the children who loved to gather around to hear them. He told them how Adonai, the one true God, who created all the earth and all the stars of heaven, placed the stars just in the right place so that they would tell a story. Pointing to a group of stars, he would have the children tell him what they represent, and after they had exhausted their guessing, he would begin his story.

This particular night it was on the famous warrior, whose belt was the Orion, and how he would put his foot on the head of the dragon chasing the famous beautiful lady of all the universe, whom the warrior loved. Valiantly the warrior would fight against the great lion, the dragon, and the bull, all for the heart of the beautiful maiden. With each character of the story, Hezron pointed to the different parts of the sky. Showing them where to look for the villains, the girl, and the how, when the moon is at the maiden's feet, and she has twelve crowns on her head, that will make it the time for the valiant warrior to marry his bride. The children loved the story; every night, Hezron would elaborate on the theme with new tales about each of the characters. Hezron knew the stories of the scrolls so well that he could easily see their fulfillment in the events of the tribes of Israel since that time. He used those stories and pointed them out in the stars for the children to all have a reference point to his story.

Late that night, a neighboring band of thieves and cutthroats raided the caravan, scattering the people, and Hezron made for the hills with a woman and child who had been serving him food and shelter while he had been staying with them. Now with the tent on fire, the caravan people scattered. Three of them headed off into the night to the hills, which was about as far away as they could go in the dark. Finding a cave, they crawled in for the night. In the distance, they could still hear the odd scream and the sound of metal against metal as the swordplay continued in sporadic moments. He lost his horse and could barely escape with his meager belongings and the scroll.

The following day, they returned to see what remained of the caravan, who was left alive, bury the dead, and start to gather up their belongings. The woman begged him to stay with her, be his husband, and father to her child. He returned her to her relatives untouched. He declared he was on a mission from the Lord and was dedicated to fulfilling his commission. If afterward, should their paths cross, he promised her, he would be more than happy to settle down with her as his wife and raise her child as his own. She wailed and cried, pleading at his feet, but to no avail. Hezron's mind was set.

Hezron knew that he needed to write down all that he had experienced and all that had transpired so that they would have a record of it. This pleased the rag-tag caravan band as they had come to love him and his stories very much, and soon he was provided with all the resources he needed to focus on writing his story and what he knew. The woman continued to serve him and take care of him, hoping that he would come to love and see that she was a good mate for him, and her father encouraged her to do so. Hezron kept his promise to write his story and tell them stories out of the scroll at night, teaching them in the ways of Adonai, in the ways of Melchizedek order.

They knew that he would not be staying, and with this scroll, they would be able to have the record, so they were content. Hezron faithfully wrote all that had transpired while staying with the caravan. He recorded all that he knew about the tribe that made war on the caravan and how he ended up with them. When he got to the part where he was going to make a copy of the actual scroll. He felt convinced that this was not a scroll for them to have. He prayed about it. But the more he implored, the more he was convinced that he needed to get it to Jerusalem. Did not the inkwell run dry? Why were they constantly interrupting him? At the time of the full moon, he went outside to see that the sky had an unusual gray sheen with lights dancing in the north where the moon had entered the stars of Pisces, the fishes. "Was it a sign?" they asked.

"It is time to pray and repent," was all he said and returned to see if the scroll could tell him more.

Later that night, when all was quiet, he left. He watched to make sure that they all were asleep. Across the desert, heading for the land, he determinedly walked, heading to where the scroll belonged. He left the travel journal he had written for them with them, including some of what was figured out from the scroll, and he believed it was for them.

Hezron stayed that night in a little village just outside of Shamai Sina. There he was invited to eat with an El-Ruag family. They had a little boy who was very curious and wanted Hezron to tell him a story after the evening meal. So Hezron told a story as he pointed upward into the sky of a virgin called Virgo who is going to give birth to a son when the moon passes between her legs and the eleven stars of Joseph's crown upon her head. The little boy is excited and points to the eleven stars and tells Hezron that one of those stars belongs to his family. His family can trace their line back to one of Joseph's sons. Patting him on the back Hezron rejoices with him, for he too belongs to one of the families in the stars. "Lamed Shin Mem," he said, nodding at his father and turning to Hezron, "have you mastered the task of separating and ruling?"

"It is the winds of the eagle, Altair, the very bright star that means the wounding or, as my Persian friend calls it, Al Cair, the piercing of the goat." Nodding his head, he again turns to the son to finish his story. "… There, he will grow to be a great archer who will battle the scorpion, who is out to place a deadly sting on the archer just as the archer draws his bow," he said, ending the story at its most exciting part.

Father laughed and said, "Time for bed," shooing them off. Turning to Hezron, after the child kissed his father goodnight and politely thanked Hezron for the lovely story, he explained why he interrupted the story. "I am most interested in what you have learned, and knowing that you are knowledgeable and patient with my child, I wanted to hear for myself what you know. Forgive me."

"Ahhh, my friend, "Hezron said with kind consideration," no need to forgive. I humbly ask your forgiveness for overstepping my bounds on your family, and I should not be telling the story to your child without your permission."

"You are most forgiven," the father acknowledged, "what do you know of the mo'adhims?"

"Adonai, our most gracious Lord, allowed me but a peek at the appointed assemblies of the stars and a little as to their meaning. To which I am humbly honored. We are here in the time of the house of lucky ones of the slaughters in which the ten captives are held in the left hand of Capricornus. That only leaves two tribes, and it breaks my heart to see this. May it be God's will that the ten not be lost," Hezron said and modestly bowed.

"The fish found in Pisces lives in the waters that flow. The twins Pisces are bound together until the sacrifice of the goat atones for their freedom," the father acknowledged. Then asked, "wise and wisdom from above has come upon you and blessed you with the story unfolding of the stars. Still, I have to ask you what sign will we know that it is time?"

"When the tail of the goat sweeps before Narubi," Hezron answered.

"Nairobi, the feared winged one?" questioned the father.

"We are not at the time of his visit, and blessed be the Lord, we are safe from his wicked days. Besides, his wife is both attracted and repelled by him, and she is the one who follows him at a safe distance and out of sight. She will come to light and gain her strength to stand in the way of any wickedness the winged one is about to do," Hezron explained.

"Ahh, you have done much to fill my mind with wonder. May you rest here while I ponder all that you have told me," the father said as he pointed to a comfortable place to rest.

Hezron spent the next few months traveling towards Jerusalem with them. Then they parted company amid tears and pleadings. Hezron knew his time with them had come to a close, he would miss them, and he promised to remember them in his prayers, as they had become like brothers in their time together.

He now avoided caravans by keeping a safe distance but always within eyesight as they traveled across the desert. Since his bad experience with traveling merchants was not something he would like to repeat, he still did trust their knowledge of the safest routes through the desert. Trying to marry him off to one of their women was a burden upon his heart that he did not want to contend with.

He would volunteer to help sheep herders in return for food and lodging and spent many nights out with the herd when he ran across them. Feeling weariness in his bones, he moved on, ever coming closer to his destination. Fighting hunger, desert winds, and so tired and weary to the bone one night, he found a cave to lay down. It tore at his heart that he was unable to finish the mission he had set out to complete. With great sadness, he took the scrolls, placed them in the satchel, and prayed that they would be found in God's time by the right people. Hezron drifted off quietly into the eternal sleep of the dead when the world grew silent with evening air.

Chapter 23

James was worried; somewhere up north was his boy and his newfound friend, and because of the lack of communication, he had no idea if he was ok or where he was. Last night's lightning show in the north didn't help with his worries either. Turning towards Johan, he said, "How about letting me take some pictures of the tablet at different angles? My son has a friend who is an astrophysicist student, and maybe he can make some sense of that circle within a winged circle. Besides, I really do need to be heading out. I have arranged to meet him in Jerusalem, and I should get going." After taking a few pictures of what Professor Goldberg discovered, he wished his friend well and was getting ready to head out, but his vehicle would not start.

One of the locals was a mechanic and went to work on it but was soon shaking his head. In his broken English, he explained, "Some vehicles have not been working since last night, especially the newer models. I have no idea how to fix them." Taking the oil rag to wipe his hands, he went on to say, "Older models that do not have computer chips were working."

James asked, "So you know of anyone willing to sell me their vehicle?"

The mechanic pointed to an old rusty vehicle behind his shop and said," I could sell you this one, but only if you include the car you have."

James shook his head and told him, "It is a rental car, and the company will be informed where they can come and pick it up once I get my phone back up and operating." After some more haggling, the mechanic let James have the old car for a price.

After a quick engine check over by the mechanic to make sure that it was suitable for the road, James waved bye and was chugging off with a puff of smoke and belch from the old car and putt-putting his way down the road.

This car was not going very fast, and it soon became apparent to James that it might not make the journey. Chugging up the hill in first gear gave new meaning to the need for prayer because, as far as he could see, this vehicle needed all the blessings it could get and someone pushing it up hills.

At the next town, he was able to trade the vehicle for a horse, figuring that it would at least be able to keep going on grass and water, which might be easier to obtain than gas. He was able to join a group of travelers and refugees heading in the same direction and soon fell into conversation with an Egyptian grad student majoring in electrical engineering. While riding side by side on horseback, they talked about the other night when all the electrical systems when down.

He explained to the Professor the workings of an electromagnetic pulse, which he believed to be the reason for the shutdown of all the electrical systems. "I believe what we have seen is something called a geomagnetic storm. These solar flares we have been experiencing have caused what is known as a solar wind which, when it strikes the earth's magnetic field, is like a shock wave hitting the earth. This solar wind changes pressure and modifies the earth's electrical currents. These storms can last up to 24-48 hours and sometimes for days, so I would not be surprised if we get hit with another one."

James thought back to a vague memory and queried, "Didn't a magnetic storm hit North America back in the 80s and disrupt power up around northeastern Canada, if my memory serves me right."

The student smiled at the Professor. He was enjoying this moment as an instructor to the Professor." You are correct. When it hit the power grid, it was only a matter of seconds as the equipment protection relays trips in a sequence of cascading events within that grid. I believe this one is more worldwide, and we will see a collapse of our twenty-first-century lifestyle."

James, leaning left then right, trying to get comfortable in the saddle, asked, "So is there anything we should be on the lookout for?"

"Intense solar flares release very high energy particles that can cause radiation poisoning in humans. The geomagnetic field does affect the biological systems. During the last storm, many birds crashed because their dependence on internal biological compasses hampering their navigational abilities. I do not know much more as it was only a tiny part of my school's general course study. I think you will find some satellites are up. We should have satellite communications available to us as they pass.

Our way. Do you have a global cell phone?" the student looking over at James, asked.

James, smiling, reached into his pocket and said, "Never leave home without it."

"When the satellite orbits are within range, your cell phone should start working again. You will find that at certain times in the day, the phone will work," he said, thinking about his own, which had given out on him as his battery died earlier.

James leaned forward. "Are you saying that this phone will work sometime soon?" he asked, reaching back into his backpack to pull out his solar phone charger and hook it up.

"I believe that you will find that it will be only good to communicate with those on similar satellite frequency. Do you have an adapter for mine?"

James looked over at the type of connection needed and shook his head. "Sorry, it is only fortunate for my son and me that solar dependency is pretty standard in our equipment because of our type of work. Something my son got me into on our last research trip."

"I couldn't tell you when or if there is a satellite will be available for you, though," the student said with a shrug.

James smiled at him. "Don't matter. Thanks for the tip. You see, I have been worried about my son. That would be great to be able to call him when it does work, because my son is coming to meet me, and he has the same global cell phone with the same company as I do. So if it works for me, it should work for him as we should be getting the satellite communication about the same time."

"Well, keep watching your bars. That should be a good indication as to when you could try to reach him," the student said before moving on to be with his family.

When the earth started to shake and rumble, the sand shifted. The animals cried out in fright and tried to run away. Everyone was scrabbling to secure the animals, the children, and supplies. The rumblings and shakings continued off and on into the night. By morning the landscape had changed. When the earthquakes started, hills and valleys of sand and earth were now nothing but flat land as far as the eye could see. Landmarks were gone.

The shaking and rippling of waves of sand as the earth quaked through the night and now morning had come with everyone shaking the sand out of everything, digging out their supplies, and surveying the land to see the devastation. It was like some giant had sifted the sand, exposing rocks and leveling the hills. They packed up their belongings after having something to eat and headed up to coast to Taba on the border with Israel and Jordon. There James parted company and headed toward the Israeli border.

The border patrol was not allowing very many people to cross the border, the line was long, and the people were hot, hungry, and getting frustrated. Some were refugees from the neighboring village, which had been hit by a tsunami. They had fled with what little they could salvage. He heard that Beer Sheva had been hit by an earthquake and the border patrol warned everyone to choose a different route to Jerusalem. It was later that evening when it came James' turn to cross the border. They questioned him quite extensively on his purpose and finally did grant him permission to pass.

He headed out to the nearest site that he knew of. He was able to find accommodation in Advert. True, it was nothing more than archeological remains of an ancient road caravan station called Nabatean, but it was a shelter for the night. There was water and grass for his horse. After settling for the night, James dug out his map and worked out how he would proceed from here. He figured he could make it to Mamshit or Memphis the next day. True, it was a national park, but he hoped that no one would bother him staying there the night. These solar storms had affected everything, and chances were that there would be no one there, not a tourist nor any national park security. He planned on staying overnight at the park's Nabatean khan.

Chapter 24

Sam was able to find some indications from various people along the way, saying that the American fitting the description that Sam gave them was seen and heading towards the border. Since Sam had no choice but to follow the leads he was given, he headed to the border.

He was able to hitch a ride with a camel driver and figured that since most automobiles were out of commission, the Professor was having similar luck and traveling just as primitively as he was. At the border, the lineup was long, hot, and muggy wait. Upon talking to the border patrol, when it was finally his turn,. They did indicate that they had seen a fellow fitting the description heading off in a north-easterly direction away from the group that he came with. So Sam purchased one of the camels from the owner and headed in the direction the patrol had given him.

Coming up on the crest, Sam got off the camel and, taking out his binoculars, looked over the ancient city to see if he could spot any activities. Off in the distance on the west side of an old stone wall was the Professor crouched, looking as if he was digging at one of the stones. Deciding that he had no real excuse for coming upon the exact location as the Professor, Sam thought it would be safer to watch from a distance.

There was no shelter to be found anywhere near where he was, so he had the camel lay down, and he threw a blanket over both the camel and himself, making a small shelter from the wind that was increasing in strength with every minute that went by. It was a dust storm that blanketed everything. When it was over, Sam would have found himself buried if it wasn't for the camel getting up, and he knew that would have been big trouble. He surveyed the landscape and saw that the Professor was doing the same. It seems as if the Professor was better off sheltered by the stone walls than he was. It looked like the Professor lost his horse during the storm, for it was nowhere to be seen. Watching from a safe distance, he observed the Professor walk the southern then westerly directions in what looked like he was hoping to get a glimpse of his horse.

Sam deliberated between coming to the rescue or continuing to watch from a distance. Bam, flashes of light danced before his eyes, a searing pain went to the kidneys, and then full body assault was on before he got his wits about him. The last thing he remembered seeing was the faces of his attackers as one of them kicked him in the head, and then it was lights out.

Three Arabian thieves had snuck up behind him, stolen his camel and all his supplies, and after a severe beating, left him dead. It was a couple hours later when the Professor came upon Sam's body after climbing the nearest high point on the easterly side to get his bearings and to see if he could spot his horse. Sam was unconscious, bruised and battered, and in no condition to even move.

Slowly Sam regained consciousness, with the Professor wiping his brow with a wet cloth. With all his years of military training, he quickly concluded that every bone in his body hurt, and all he could do was moan as he slowly regained some cognitive skills as to his whereabouts and recent memories of the fight. He slowly opened his eyes to see the Professor calling his name.

Professor James spotted him in the desert and immediately recognized him as a seat partner on his flight. Upon checking him over, he found the man to be more bruised and banged up than anything. Only when Sam regained enough to verify 'ok to move'; did James feel relief. Carefully, he lifted the man onto his feet and supported him as they made their way down the hill to the only shade that could be found under an outcropping over a rock overhang.

James spent the rest of the day tending to his wounds and scavenging for anything to eat, drink, or use for shelter. By the end of the day, he had accumulated some of his backpack belongings, some of Sam's belongings, which included snack bars and a canister of water which he used sparingly, not knowing how long it would be before they found more water.

It was later that night the earthquake started. It shook in waves rippling across the sandy desert. Hanging on to a rock outcropping and supporting Sam on the rock, James could wait out the quaking. Wave after wave of sand rolled across the landscape like the ocean waves breaking on the beach. Then just as soon as it had started, it was over. The land was flat now, with outcroppings of rocks to dot the landscape as far as the eye could see.

Most of the foundation and walls of the remains were now buried in the sand. James made a mental note to return with an archeological team and authorization to do an official study of the site. Even the wall of Nabatean khan was not much more than a nudge on the landscape, and another earthquake or wind storm could bury it completely. Gone off the map of human history and out of sight in the landscape of nothing but sand.

But right now, he was more concerned about Sam. There was no telling if he had internal injuries or not. Sam was in and out of consciousness for most of the night. He moaned with every toss and turn, fitfully sleeping, while James watched over him.

It was morning, with the sun shining directly into his eyes, that Sam woke up and looked at his surroundings through squinting eyes. He noticed that James was propped up against a rock right beside him sleeping. He felt himself to make sure he was all there and to detect just how many bruises and other injuries he had sustained. It felt like the whack on the head had done the most damage. He felt like hell, with his head still throbbing. Getting slowly up and carefully so as not to upset any of the sore spots, he eased himself into a sitting position beside James with his back against the rock.

James must have felt his movement because he jolted awake and looked over to see Sam beside him. "Good morning," he said groggily.

"Nice to see you are up," Sam indulged.

James reached over to check Sam for fever. "How are you feeling?" James asked once he was done his probing and prodding of all the sorest spots on Sam's body.

"Thanks for finding me," Sam said, wishing James would stop but didn't have much energy to do anything more than jerk away and grimace every time he hit on a tender spot that seemed to be everywhere. "Feels like I was hit on the back of the head with a two-by-four," he said, painfully grinning, which didn't quite make it up to his eyes.

James was glad to see that Sam had survived the night. "Good morning to you too," he said, rolling his shoulders carefully; James asked, "What could you have possibly run into to do all this damage?"

Sam could visualize the face of the assailant. "Probably some thief, since I am now without my camel or supplies. They must have snuck up from behind and hit me over the head. I do not remember much after that, and I figure I am lucky to be alive. What day is it? How long have I been out? When did you find me?" he asked as though coming flooding back.

"I have lost track of the days, and I do not think you have been out very long since all the damage looks recent. I found you yesterday evening when I went to look for my horse. Do you remember the wind storm?" James inquired, looking into Sam's eyes to see if he could detect any brain damage. Not that he knew what he should be looking for.

"Yeah, it was shortly after that when it happened. I had just got my camel unburied from all the sand and was about to collect my stuff when I was hit from behind," Sam recollected as he gathered his thoughts.

"It seems as if we are both on foot. Where are you headed?" James asked as he looked over the landscape for signs of his horse, Sam's camel, or roving thieves that may still be in the area.

Sam tried to think of a logical excuse for being here and came up with it. "Well, I was heading to the only safe country in the Middle East for those of us who are not Muslim. I figure that the first nation to be back up and running in Israel since they are so resourceful. And you?"

James nodded. "Yes, I am going to Jerusalem to meet with my son. I have no way to reach him and just hope that he makes it there."

Sam encouraged James to tell him about his adventure since the last time they saw each other. James told Sam about his son, their newly found relationship, and the latest adventure with his son coming out to meet him. Sam changed the subject when he saw the pain it brought to James' eyes.

Since a complete search of the area did not turn up many of their belongings, and soon without food or water, they decided that the sooner they got closer to civilization, the better. It was not far before they ran into James' horse nibbling on a small tuff of grass. James gathered up the reins and soon checked the backpack for food and water.

Giving everyone a sip of the water and sharing the meager bits of food he had, Sam was placed on the horse with James leading. By calculating the sun's position, they decided that a north-westerly direction should get them close to where they were heading. There was an eerie silence as they trudged along, and there were no birds, animals, or insect sounds.

James casually commented on it to Sam, but Sam was nodding off and gave barely an "umm." Sam needed to rest, water, and get nourishment soon, or he might not make it. James was hoping to find shelter before the heat of the day. James veered off to the left when he spotted some trees in the distance. The heat was getting intense, and any shelter was better than none, and today looked like it was going to be a scorcher. Stumbling with the shirt over his head, James tried to keep going.

The horse picked up its head, snorted, and picked up the pace. James was caught off guard, jerked off his feet, and dragged as the horse started to run, with James hollering from the rough ground and speed in which the gravel was shaving his skin off his elbows and belly. Sam bobbed awake and quickly realized the situation leaning down, grabbing the reins, and helping James pull the horse around to a stop. Once the horse was under control, Sam said, "He smells water."

James reached for the stirrup and grabbed the horse to throw himself on behind Sam. "Help me up on the back of the horse. We will let him have his lead." Once given the lead, the horse quickened the pace again and was soon at the water hole under the trees. Sam slid off the horse onto the ground in an unceremonious thump. James slid off the rump of the horse and was running up and sliding head first into the water, scooping up the water with his hands to his parched lips. Sam crawled there more slowly but soon was drinking in the water with the rest of them. Not wanting to get sick from drinking too much water too soon, James pulled the horse back and tied it to a tree. James and Sam went further into the water to soak their tired and hot bodies.

James could see all the bruises Sam had on his body when he had taken off his shirt to get into the water. He was most colorful on his right shoulder, and there was definitely a lump on the back of his head. What puzzled James was why Sam's path crossed here in the middle of nowhere. He could understand Sam's explanation, but this is a big country but to have crossed his path again was incredible. Sam didn't know what to make of it. In one sense, he was glad it happened, but in another, it nagged at the back of his mind. Sam did seem to do an excellent job of looking like a local too.

James ventured, "Hey, Sam. Now that we will wait it out here until evening, why don't you tell me a little more about yourself?" As he said this, he was getting comfortable under a tree beside Sam.

Sam had been thinking about what he would tell James if it came up. He knew that the closer to the truth of his story, the easier it was to remember. "I started out in the military on the army side when I left school, and it was the best thing for me. My superiors soon determined that I had an aptitude for Intelligence, and I was transferred to covert operations during the 'desert storm.' There I was trained in survival tactics in the desert. Do you see that plant over there? It stores water in its roots, which we can eat. I once went a week in the wilderness with nothing more than a pocketknife, a flint striker, snare wire, and a small signal mirror. I lost about 20 pounds because all I could catch was one itty bitty six-inch perch. I had a handful of some grass seeds and cattail shoots to eat. I did find that I was not overly hungry after the first day. Water was my biggest worry. How about you?"

James scratching his head, shrugged his shoulders and said, "Nah, not me. I have no survival training. For the most part, I do not think about it. It is one of those things where I have always lived my life thinking it is best to figure out what is best at that moment and do it. No point in getting panicked over it. It is not going to change anything."

Sam agreed. "Yep, panic is a killer in emergency situations. It blinds a person to thought and planning, and it causes them to compound the situation and often times with fatal results. I say be constructive in your course of action. So how about if you bring over what you have in your supply kit, and we will see what we can do with it." And with that, Sam was able to start a fire, and soon they were drinking a weak flavored soup out of the leaves and roots of the plant.

James sipped on the brew. "Not bad considering what we had to work with," he said, leaning back and returning the cup to Sam to allow him a chance to get some nutrients. "I have always found that starting a fire is a calming influence, and it gives us time to consider our options."

Sam agreed and asked, "How many containers do we have with which we can carry water?"

James rifled through his bag, threw out all of the contents, and said, "That is it," revealing just a few odd things like shampoo and conditioner bottles. "Looks like we will have to forgo clean for water," he said and poured out the contents.

Sam continued to drink his brew. "How far do you think we have to go before we reach civilization?"

"I believe we could be a day away, maybe two."

James agreed. "What do you think is the best plan of action from here?" he asked as he went over to the water's edge to wash the bottles out.

Sam reached over and poured himself another drink. "Whatever we decide, let's stick to it and together get to Jerusalem." Sam felt his strength come back and settled down to rest for the long journey this evening. They had decided that evening travel would be out of the heat, and with the moon and cooler weather out tonight, they should be able to make better time.

James attended to the horse by bringing him back to the watering hole for another drink, then over to a grassy knoll beside an old stump where he could tie the horse down. He joined Sam for some much-needed rest and attendance to the raw skin spots on his body. Once salved, relief came, and James was able to find a comfortable position under the trees.

Both had dozed off, and when the chill of the evening air hit their bodies, they were aroused and refresh. It didn't take long to gather up their meager belongings and load up the horse for the journey. Sam had to be convinced that he was not yet up to the long walk and would be riding with James leading. From the map Sam had, they had determined that they were still quite a few miles away from Jerusalem but hoped to reach it by morning.

Chapter 25

Travis drove while John slowly pulled the scroll out of the satchel, being very careful to not damage it. This scroll was in remarkable condition, not even very brittle, which was strange, written on what looked to be either goatskin or lambskin. It was treated with a final film of waxy material. It seemed to have been its protection from the elements all these years. The scroll looked ancient. Peeking in, his eyes caught sight of the lettering. Aramaic, if his guess was correct. There was a word here and there that he knew for sure, but for the most part, he could not decipher much of what he saw. It looked like this would be a job for his father. Just then, Travis hit a bump, and John realized how foolish it was to be handling the scroll now. He asked Travis to pull over so he could secure the scroll back in the satchel and in a safe place before they proceeded any further. Once safe, Travis got back on the road and started to pick up the pace. Pushing the truck to an even faster rate, the truck protested with high-pitched engine whining.

"Kwpowww wap wap wap" the front tire swerved the truck to the left and almost off the road. Travis slammed on the brakes with both hands firmly on the steering wheel, fighting to regain control, and skidded to a stop. Travis hopped out of the truck to change the tire.

Looking up, John seeing Travis had everything back under control, said, "I will rest my eyes as I see you have everything under control."

"Yes, I have everything under control. You rest your eyes, and you have my assurance that your help will not be needed," Travis retorted sarcastically. John snickered from under his hat.

While Travis worked on the tire, a cinder flew onto his shirt, causing him to jump. He brushed it off. Hit with another live flame looks up towards the direction they came from. At that moment, he saw a lot more coming and called for John to get under the truck. Travis scrambled to get under before any more hits.

John's immediate thought was the scroll and scrambling to get it and himself under the truck. They waited until the storm was over, hoping the vehicle would not catch fire. Just as soon as the fiery hail storm stopped, they were out from under the truck and quickly working on putting out the fires. John's passenger seat was severely burned, and he had to put his backpack in the hole for a seat cushion. It looked like it took the biggest hit.

Happy that it was brief and didn't cause more significant damage, they quickly finished putting the spare tire on and heading down the road again. John secured the satchel up behind the heater unit of the truck against the firewall on the passenger side, where it could not be seen as a precaution.

They were almost at the Israeli border and hoped that John's father was in Jerusalem to greet them. It had been days since their last communication, and even though John kept checking his phone, there was no signal. Travis was always amused when John set up the little solar power unit to keep the cell phone working. He was glad that John and his father had the solar chargers, and they would probably be one of the few that did. With what was going on with the solar flares, taking out all the electrical grids in the world would not surprise Travis. John had mentioned once that because archeological sites are usually pretty remote, there were a lot of items that are unique to self-sufficiency that John possessed.

Travis figured that since the fiery hailstorm could have come from an extraordinary solar flare. This one was a gathering electrified storm that peppered the planet with particles so energized that they caught fire upon entering the earth's atmosphere and were large enough to still be burning when they touched the ground.

Just as they crested the hill, they saw the border crossing below. It was strange to see just a couple of horses and a couple of men guarding the border, but with what was going on with the atmosphere, it made sense. It wasn't long before they reached the border. The men were questioning them as to how they were able to have a vehicle running. Travis explained to them as he was passing over their passports that this vehicle was pre-computer electronics and was not affected by the solar flares. With a thorough search of their vehicle and numerous questions about their being so far from home, they were allowed to pass. The border patrol did laugh at the tin foil on the motor when they saw it. Travis blushed, and John laughed with them at his discomfort. They were glad that the satchel was not found, for they knew they could not adequately explain how it got into their possession.

They figured they would stay at Nazareth, the closest town across the border. They were tired, it was getting late, and they were ready for food and rest. As they entered the city, they noticed it was strangely quiet.

The gunfire came at them from both sides. They ducked low and kept moving. They felt like sitting ducks with their old truck putting along. The gunfire came behind them on those who had been taking potshots at them. With odd shots in their direction, most of it was now diverted back to where other gunfire was coming from. Once they got around the corner, they again found it eerie quiet. They were very watchful and still slunk down low in the truck. But it looked like they were now entering the Israeli section of town.

Pulling up to the first hotel they came across, they went in to secure a room. They were informed that there would be cold running water, no electricity, and thus no conveniences like television. This they acknowledged was fine, just as long as they could find some food. The desk clerk pointed down the street and said that while you may purchase some food in the local market, there would be no way to prepare it. So choose food that you want to eat as is. With that, they unloaded their bags on the bed once they got up to their room and took turns having a brisk cold quick shower to get some of the dirt off. Feeling refreshed, they both ventured out to see what food they could find. On the street corner, they found one old man had set up a little burner and had a stew brewing. They were able to purchase some breadfruit and two bowls of stew. It satisfied their hunger, and with a couple more purchases of dry goods that could be eaten cold and stored well, they returned to their rooms for the night.

Chapter 26

James had this nagging thought come back at the back of his mind that Sam was not on the up and up. The coincidence that he happened to be on the same plane and now show up again here in the middle of nowhere just didn't add up. They had not made it as far as they had hoped but were fortunate enough to find a shepherd out watching his sheep and with both of them using what knowledge they had of the Hebrew language were able to have to shepherd lead them to a stream sheltered by hills. There they settled in for the night with the shepherd and his flock.

The earth started shaking again, forcing them to lay sprawled out, hoping to ride it out. The earthquakes were increasing in frequency and lasting longer than James had experienced in California. The way they moved across the landscape reminded him that these were not like plate shifting but more like ripples. He wondered why these felt different. Then it was over. Getting up and dusting themselves off, they went about the task of gathering everything up again. They helped the shepherd find missing sheep and found one lamb had died. This the shepherd quickly skinned and cut up into pieces to throw on the fire for that night's meal.

As he was moving slowly around the camp, Sam picked up this and that item and asked, "So tell me more about this thing you are looking for?"

James responded as he picked up the backpack and dusted it off. "It is a scroll that may have come from the Alexandria library before it burned to the ground, and there is some indication that it may be still in existence."

Sam pushed further with, "Do you have any idea about the scroll itself?"

James was beginning to feel like he was being quizzed just a little too much and mumbled, "Haven't a clue."

Sam said, "What about its subject matter?"

James just shook his head and said, "Nope." Sam backed off, laughing,

"So you are on a wild goose chase?" Sam asked, trying to recover with a light-hearted comment. He knew that the Professor was not telling him all that he knew about the scroll, and somehow he lost the Professor's confidence in confiding in him.

James muttered, "Could be." With that, he started walking off to fetch the horse and bring it in for its evening watering. James had decided that at the first opportunity once they reached Jerusalem, to lose Sam.

The following day they bid farewell to the shepherd, and with some cooked lamb left over from the night before given generally by the shepherd as his way of saying thanks for helping gather his sheep, they headed out with Sam on the back of the horse and James again walking. By mid-morning, it was becoming evident that Sam was feeling a lot better because he even offered to walk a piece and let James ride for a while. That did soften up the Professor's mood a bit towards Sam. Soon they were back to talking with Sam telling stories from his life as a marine.

"I have to tell you that when I was first recruited, it was in the wee dark hours of the morning that I stepped off that bus into a whole new world. I think my mind went into shock or cardiac arrest because that drill sergeant was the most sadistic, maniacal tyrant I had ever encountered. It was beyond my comprehension that something like that could come in human form, and no one had ever treated me like that before. And it was my daily struggle to survive. In fact, I think that I was beginning to wonder as the days went on whether I was neurotic to even allow such a psychopath to be in charge of my life or live another day. Eventually, my mind went numb, and my weary, spent body literally just died each night, wishing it would not wake up. You could say I was living in limbo during that time period."

"So why did you continue?" James asked, encouraging Sam to continue.

"I guess for me, it was that moment where it all of a sudden clicks that it matters. For me, it was one week before graduation when I would finally be a United States Marine. I was at the end of three months of sweat, pain, and hard work. It was in the Final Drill completion. I can still hear the Drill Sergeant's instructions echoing across the wide expanse of asphalt. 'Column left, Harrrch!' 'Extend, Haarch!' 'Poort, Arms!' and only Marines Sergeants can march a platoon with such command and precision. From our razor-sharp uniforms to our stone-cold piercing eyes, dedication and honor oozed out of our pores as we snapped to a halt. Our platoon was good, and we knew it. We had perfectly executed our drill sequence as if we had lived for this moment. I was in the third squad and in the second rank. The drill sergeant hollered, 'Column of files from the right, Haaarch' Each squad stepped off, and then it was my turn to step off.

"I was doing some daydreaming as I went through the routine. My mind was on going home, where a brand new pickup truck was waiting for me. I imagined that, with my Marine uniform, strutting around back home, I would get some respect and ohh, the girls I would meet." Shaking his head, Sam acknowledged, "Reality struck. When I came to my senses, it was too late. I had just messed up. The Drill Sergeant was in my face, screaming, 'Wake up. As I woke up from my daydreaming, I realized those words cut really deep. This man in front of me embodied everything I ever imagined a Marine to be, and he taught me so much. He was a Marine, and I let him down in the worst way. His passion was to be the best with the most well-disciplined platoon, who knew the art of Close Order Drill - the Marine way. But more than that, it was the shame of 'being the one" as the Marine Corps says 'there is always the one who doesn't want to follow the rules. There is always the one who screws it up for the rest of the unit. There is always one who gets others killed in battle. From that moment on, I vowed never to be that 'one' again. At that time, I wished the entire incident could be rewound and done over correctly. But I will never forget that hard lesson learned that day, it will always be fresh in my mind, and I have been dedicated to the task before me since then."

"So, what is your task now?" James asked.

Sam paused, looked around him as if waking up and frowning, and said, "You know, up to this moment, I have only given the current solar storms and the havoc they have played on our planet as a minor setback. But now that you ask, this may be more than a minor setback, and what I came to Egypt for may no longer have any future. I guess you could say my life is on pause until we see how much this world can recover when this storm is over."

"Well, in my field, preservation of what we did have will always have a role in our world's future and its knowledge. I will always be in pursuit of past civilizations and their knowledge," James acknowledged with quiet comfort in his purpose in life.

The miles were eaten up with stories; before long, they were at the crest of the hill looking down on what should have been Jerusalem. What was before their eyes were what looked like a city devastated by an earthquake. The fire marked different parts of the town, and rubble marked other parts. Sections were still standing. But famous landmarks like the Temple Mount, Basilica of Agony, Church of the Holy Sepulcher, and The old city from the Jewish quarters to the Way of the Cross were all lying in ruins. James was stunned and, with his mouth hanging open, just looked down, saying nothing. Sam, equally stunned at the devastation but quicker to recover as he had seen much destruction in his days, turned to see how James was handling the site.

James was slowly sliding down off the horse and stumbling down the hill. Sam followed silently behind, leading the horse. Coming through the old part of the city, they went into Mahane Yehuda, the kind of outdoor marketplace usually teeming with people marketing all types of fish, meats, and other eatables along with odds and ends. This place today was bare of supplies upon which a person could stock up on supplies. Sam and James were able to purchase enough supplies to satisfy their current hunger, eating as they made their purchases. Usually, Jerusalem is a beautiful city to explore because of the many monumental critical historical sites, but today even the Shrine of the Book, where the fragments of the Dead Sea Scrolls were in ruins with the odd looter being chased by guards. But obviously, not enough guards were available to protect the masterpieces and artifacts from the many looters. James shakes his head in sadness, knowing that some of the archaeological relics at this particular museum had been dated back as far as the Early Stone Age. Patriots of Judea were defending the site against the Islamic faction who was bent destroying on its collection of Judaic archeological material. As a skirmish between the two factions broke out as they were forty yards past where the building once was, Sam didn't need to urge the horse forward as it took off down the street.

Poor James was doing his best to keep up but tripped, landing in the dust. Sam quickly secured the horse around the corner and ran back, darting between one object and another until he was by James' side. "You ok?" he asked upon skidding in beside James. James wiggled to see if all was in working order and nodded. Sam peeked around the edge of the concrete block obscuring them from open fire.

The Israeli forces were currently driving the Islamic group back towards their left flank, thus opening a way for them to weave their way back to where their horse was. Grabbing the Professor, he motioned for James to follow him, keeping low and waiting for his signals. With quick instructions, Sam explained a few key signs and gave strict instructions to do what he signaled when he signaled. With that, Sam peeked out and assessed the situation. An opening to the left behind a turned-over burning vehicle was pointed out to James. James was given the instructions to run, which James did with flinching at each round of gunfire. Sam was not far behind and again checked around the end at the bumper for the next opening to run. Together they bolted this time but seemed to have gathered no attention, so Sam kept them moving from one cover to the next until they were able to round the corner only to see some kid making off with their horse. Sam gave chase, hollering at the boy to give back his horse.

Sam chased him past the Knesset, Israel's parliament, past the impressive bronze menorah given to the Israeli government as a gift from the British government. The Israeli Supreme Court building was now in ruins and had once been acclaimed for its contemporary architecture. Through what once was a beautiful garden, Gan Havradim, there was still an odd rose or two trying to color its spot with beauty. Obviously, the boys didn't know how to ride, or they would have been alight of the horse by now, Sam thought. The boys headed out of the center of town up Herzl Street past memorial park and cemetery. At the graveyard, the boys trying to weave their way through slowed down enough for Sam to catch up. With one final burst of energy, Sam grabbed the reins out of the one boy's hand and caught the boy's shirt by the scruff of the neck. The other boy bolted. The boy he had grabbed went into an all-out wild flinging of his body to wrench himself free, scaring the horse into furiously backing up from the flailing boy and stretching Sam's arms to their limit. Sam let go of the boy to regain control of the horse, and by the time Sam had control of the situation, the boy was long gone. Sam retraced his steps with the horse back to where he had left the Professor, only to find him gone.

"Awww crap!" Sam said as he viciously kicked the nearest object. Stubbing his toe, he yelped in pain, hopping around, holding not only the horse but now his foot. Gathering everything, he lost the Professor, who happened to be carrying his satchel at the time of the incident.

Chapter 27

James watched Sam chase after the boy and horse and waited until he saw that he went around the corner. Looking down at the satchel at the boy's feet, with a shrug picked it up. He then headed out in the opposite direction. He had not lost anything but the horse. But now was his opportunity to lose Sam. With that, he turned towards the Historical and Art Museums where he was to meet his son at the Yad Vashem, a place where tribute was paid to courageous non-Jews for risking their own lives to save Jews from certain death. It was there John had been instructed to place a note under a rock at the foot of the Talmudic inscription: "Whoever saves a single soul, it is as if he had saved the entire world," as to where James could find where his son was staying in case communication was still down. Looking around, he didn't find a note, so he left one of his own telling John that he would be back here tomorrow at noon, dated it and signed his name, and laid it under a rock at the foot of Yad Vashem.

With that, James headed to his favorite little bed and breakfast place in the heart of the city center, the Jerusalem Inn. It was an old hotel with deep roots in Jerusalem-style hospitality and brought up fond memories as James neared where it was located. Turning onto Horkanos Street, James was saddened to see part of the building was down. Edging closer, he walked through the door to have a look-see. There was a young man at the desk, and as he approached, he asked if any rooms were available.

The young man nodded and explained. "While there was no electricity and parts of the building had been destroyed, I do have some rooms available with cold running water if you are interested."

James assured him, "That would be fine." After paying a ridiculous price for the room, he was instructed to the second floor by the broken section. Cracks in the wall, plaster coming off in spots, and a broken window was boarded up. Otherwise, the room was intact. Beggars can't be choosers, James thought to himself as he threw his knapsack on the bed and proceeded to the bathroom to clean up not only his clothes but his body. Using the sink for his laundry and later the curtain rod from the shower for his clothes hanger, he felt clean. It was not long before James was comfortable again under the covers, as he had no other clean clothes, with his papers before him snacking on fruit and bread and drinking some wine he had purchased.

Chapter 28

Rumbling and gas spewing forth from the cracks in the earth intensified. Earthquakes shook the ground beneath Travis and John's vehicle the following day as they headed out. It shook so hard, and the air sizzled as fire flicked across the sky. Travis scrambled out of the truck, hollering at John to get out. John grabbed the bag out from behind the heater, while Travis grabbed their backpacks from behind the seats. They both were thrown as the truck exploded from an electrical overload like a bomb in the gas tank. Both were thrown clear. There they lay on the ground until the earthquake stopped with hands over their heads, praying.

John checked the satchel first to make sure nothing was damaged before checking himself to see if he was hurt. Travis was up first, scanning the sky and landscape to see if he saw any signs of anything more about to happen. Once re-assured, he dusted himself off and went to go find his hat, gather up what belongs he could find, and go look for John. One glance told him the truck was toast. Nothing but a bonfire spitting and hissing. A tire popped loudly. Travis jumped and watched air gush forth before quickly deflating completely. Travis scanned the rest of the truck to see if anything else going to go off before calling out to John. Turning his head away, one of the gas cans in the back exploded, sending Travis diving. The can landed just a few feet in front of them, getting both to scramble to their feet and run a little distance away from the burning vehicle.

Picking themselves up and dusting off any burning embers, they checked their bags to make sure they were OK and glanced around to see how the rest of the terrain looked. The land was getting flatter with every earthquake.

Travis shook his head and said, "It is only going to get worse."

Cutting his eyes at Travis, John pursed his lips in a scowl and, with a big breath out, said, "Ya' think?" with all the sarcasm he could muster.

Travis cracked a dimpled smile and then laughed. With his infectious laugh, he soon had John joining him. Tension seeped from their bodies, and when they both caught their breath, they started to laugh again. It was just nerves. Wiping a tear from the corner of his eye with his sleeve, Travis soberly said, "Ya' I think," which sobered John up quickly.

"OK, tell me, what do you know about all this solar storm stuff? And just how much of it do we have to look forward to?" John stared intently at Travis.

"My theory is that the Niribu is causing the solar storms. It is trying to break free of the magnetic field of our sun. Right now, it is on the other side of the sun, and the effect it has had on the sun for over three years is stopping the sunspots from occurring by the magnetic pull it is having on the molten lava on the sun. Something like the moon has on our earthly ocean waves. With every effort to one side of the sun, we get sprayed with solar fires and earthquakes. Once it is free of the sun's magnetic field, which I believe it will, if this last episode is any indication, we are in for a severe magnetic field pull from Niribu as it comes our way." Travis watched John digest that piece of information.

"Back up a moment and tell me who or what is a Niribu?" John fired back Travis took a deep breath and asked, "Have you ever heard of planet X?"

Exasperated, John said, "Why don't you just get to the point and tell me?" He started to get a little frustrated at what he was beginning to think that getting information out of Travis was like pulling teeth, painful.

Putting his hand up in mock surrender, he quietly motioned him to walk beside him as he started to tell him what he knew. "Niribu is a recently discovered binary planet that enters our solar system every 3600 years. Binary in that while it is the main planet, it does have a more minor planet that seems to have a serious pull on it, creating an erratic travel pattern. Think of it this way, imagine you have two round objects on each end of rubber bands. One with more weight but the other smaller with enough to jerk it in another direction. So that while its travel pattern is elliptical, it is leapfrogging with trajectory forces each other. Since most believe the other is a little brown dwarf star, it does not get much recognition, including not even having its own name. Niribu, on the other hand, could mostly be made up of weighty magnetic material, which gives it a solid gravitational force with all planets that cross its path. But I already told you that. I believe that we can expect it to break free from the sun's gravitational pull any day now and head our way."

"Why?" John stopped to look, quizzing Travis.

"It was some calculations that a learned professor and I worked on one night recently at his place. Based on his knowledge and is vast on this subject. I would say that we are in for the biggest earthquake, volcanic eruptions, and tsunamis this world has ever experienced." Travis was about to continue with something about trajectory and calculations when John abruptly cut him off.

"Get to the point," John said and started walking again. Travis picked up the pace and was soon beside him.

Shifting his backpack, Travis once again picked up his thoughts with, "The planet is one bigger than our earth, two. We are talking about being bigger than Saturn. Three of the reasons that it has not been spotted is its pull on space itself. To such an extent, there was talk that it was a black hole for a while. That is why it was not seen, but now I have a different theory. I believe that whatever it is made up of, it attracts with a gravitational and a light force. It actually bends the light around it, thus rendering it sometimes invisible. Only when it comes in contact with debris do we even get a reflection of the wings of its speed and gravitational force. Thus the darkness in the middle lights up like a fire giving the planet itself a red glow, "he said. Stopping again, Travis pulled out the printed NASA website sheets of the solar eclipses and their dates and locations of appearing. Pointing to the chart, he said, "If my theory is correct, we will have a very long and growing blackness over the sun as it swings out from behind. It will look like a winged moon eclipse, which glows red. But this one will not be. As it approaches, it will increase its forces upon the earth and any other object in its way," he said, rolling up the NASA website sheets and placing them back in the backpack before continuing. "What we will be experiencing is even metals which are not normally affected by magnetic forces like gold which is not known to be magnetic. I say that it is because our gold has not come into contact with this magnetic force. Some metals that are not known to be magnetic are gold, aluminum, silver, and good stainless steel."

Travis was picking up the pace as he talked passionately about the subject, and from what John could see, he was just warming up. He hurriedly tried to keep up.

Travis didn't even notice. "I have been thinking as I was driving just how we can survive Niribu, but as of yet have not come up with an answer," he said and went silently into deep thought as if John no longer existed. Suddenly, he stopped. "If we have enough eddy currents that can change the magnetic field, that net effect would be to repel electrically conductive from the alternative magnetic field. Many kinds of electrically conducting flakes, but gold is one of the better electrical conductors. At this level, we would need a concentrated amount for a focal point to redirect Niribu off our earth's magnetic field." Smiling for the first time, Travis turned to John and said, "Oh, I wish there was a way to communicate with NASA right now." And with that goes silent again. John had never seen Travis so worked up and admired how his mind worked even if he didn't understand half of what he was saying. Obviously, Travis thought he was on to something. It was not long before they were at the crest of the hill. John was the first to see Jerusalem off in the distance. At least, it should be.

It was late that night when they arrived in the city and scouted for a place to stay. It ended up that they camped out one more night in the open air, under a grove of trees in some garden somewhere. They were not the only ones, as many others were pitching tents and setting up camp in different parts of what looked to be a park.

Chapter 29

It was noon the next day when James arrived at Yad Vashem, and what to his heart did he see but his son and his newfound friend sitting at the foot resting. It brought relief to his mind as he picked up the pace, calling out, "John, hey, John."

John turned towards the voice and saw his father heading his way. He got up and ran over to give him a big hug. There they embraced, then embarrassed, quickly parted, and both started to talk at once. "It is so good to see you. I was worried about you."

"We found something we would like you to see. Do you have a place out of prying eye's view where we can show you?" John said excitedly, all in one breath. And remembered his manners as Travis approached the pair. "I would like you to meet Travis, the astrophysicist student I told you about. I find some of the stuff he is saying may help us understand the astronomy of what may be in Hezron's scroll when we find it. Did you have any luck with that?"

"Come follow me." James quickly shook Travis's hand and turned to lead them back to the Inn. "I am so glad you made it," he said, giving his son another manly side squeeze." I was beginning to worry," he said, checking John over with his eyes. "Did you experience some of the solar storms or earthquakes?" Upon seeing that, other than being a bit dirty, he looked fit. "How long have you been in town?" he asked, as he continued to rattle off questions without waiting for answers." Where are you staying?" he asked, climbing over the rubble. "Do you have any transportation?" He paused. "What have you found that needs to be out of 'prying eye's view?' he said, frowning, this time expecting an answer.

John shook his head in disbelief at the stream of questions. Travis and John shared a conspiratorial look. "To make a long story short, we have found a scroll we would like you to take a look at."

That sent the Professor into another rapid-fire volley of questions, "Where did you find it?" he asked again, turning to the task of getting to the Inn. "Did you look at it?" Picking up the pace, he said, "Did you see what is on it? How old do you think it is? Did you recognize the language? What condition is the parchment in? Is it safe? Who have you shown? Did you report this to the authorities?" And sheepishly, he stopped. "Never mind, we will get to my questions once I get you comfortably settled into the Inn where I am staying because it looks as if you have been sleeping under the stars and could use a good wash," he said, assessing the boys, "and a good meal. Then we will talk." And with that, he turned around the corner, heading into the Inn. He registered the boys for the room next to his.

Once settled in and cleaned up, John brought out the scroll for his father to look at. James was conscientious; with the tools he brought with him, he opened up the scroll and started to work on deciphering. "It looks to be ancient Aramaic writing, and from BCE, anywhere from 10 to the 6th century is my guess. Do you see this?" he asked, pointing to a specific text. "It is the word 'asah' which translates to the word 'did' a verb particular to the Hebrew language and specific to the Hebrew culture which was not adopted to other cultures until much later." And with pen and paper in hand began the work of translating. Professor James, consumed with the need to translate as much of it as he could, wrote furiously, and with John looking over his shoulder helping with the odd guess here and there, they were oblivious to Travis.

Travis seeing that they were going to be at this a while, decided that he left to go out and forage for some food and drink for everyone. As he headed out the door, he said, "I will be back with something for us to eat." But neither one of them gave him a glance. John at least provided a vague wave in his direction but never took his eyes off the manuscript. Travis laughed to himself, shaking his head. Father and son were so much alike.

When Travis arrived back, James was excited, and John, in his excitement, grabbed Travis by both shoulders to blurt in his face, "This is the missing scroll where Jeremiah tells where he hid the ark. It says here: 'The Word of the Lord came to me saying, 'Write this down and place it in a safe place, to be gathered up, when the time is right for the ark to come forth from its hiding place.'" And looking up from his notes, he said, "We are not finished with the translating, but it looks as if we have one of the greatest finds in archeological history."

Travis dropped the bag of food and grabbed the notes that John had written down so far to read all that they had translated. "These are the words of Jeremiah in the year of the reign of Josiah, king of Judah. It is the first month at the time of the new moon when the word of the Lord came to me. 'Jeremiah, you must take the ark to a safe place where I tell you, tonight under cover of darkness.' And I, struck through the heart at such a task, asked, 'oh why, Lord, must I do such a thing?' But the Lord answered me, saying, 'The disaster from the north will be poured out, and I have gathered four faithful to carry the ark where you lead them. The kings have set up their thrones. At the entrance of the gates of Jerusalem, they will come against all the towns of Judah and Jerusalem. They will destroy my Holy Temple and take all away to their homeland. I have pronounced judgments upon my people and the temple where they performed great wickedness in forsaking me, burning incense to other gods, and worshipping that which they have made with their hands. Repent, I say, repent, lay prostrate on the ground trusting in my mercy and forgiveness in a great time of trouble. The Lord is mighty to save. Trust in Him. The proud and fierce shall all be taken away. Rise up not, but wait until you see the way of salvation come upon you.

'Get yourself ready to travel wherever I command you. So be not terrified by either the wicked priest in my temple or the kings outside the gate. I have made you away, and they will not detain you or the ark from leaving. They will not fight you or overcome you, for I am with you and will rescue you,' declared the Lord," he said, reaching the end of translation.

"Wow!" said Travis as he sat down on the bed, laying the first sheet down, and reached for another sheet of paper where John had written more. "You shall find on the north side of the temple a broken lock on one of the doors, there you will meet the four men I have waiting, lead them inside the temple to the most holy, and be not afraid, for they have been chosen by me and have cleansed their souls for this task. Israel was sacred to the Lord, the first fruits of his harvest, blessed with my presence and my Holy Word. Hear the word of the Lord, tonight I will take away my blessings, I will let those they have gone after to take them away, for my Israel has been held guilty, and disaster will overtake her. This is what the Lord said. "They have strayed so far from me and have followed worthless idols and now have become worthless. They do not call upon me, The Lord who has brought them out of Egypt and led them through the barren wilderness, the land of deserts, the land of drought, and a land where no one travels and no one lives. I will call upon those of the order of Melchizedek to come forth." Travis laid down the paper and asked John, "Are we talking about the same group you were telling me about?" and looked around to see if there was any more translated.

John nodded and, seeing that he had finished reading, said, "We have not been able to make out a section because of the fragmentations, but we have been able to translate this part," handing him another sheet of paper. "This is where you might be able to help us because I believe it is getting into where the ark can be found."

Travis was impressed with the amount of translation they could do in the time they worked on it. Taking the paper from John, he read, "At this time, Michael shall stand with his right foot on the place where I had you lay the ark. It will be at a time of great distress to all the nations, like nothing that happened before. It will be at the time when it is most needed. It will come forth. They whom I have called to the task will look to Orion and the constellations to the south and watch the cords of the mighty hunter's belt loosen. I, the Lord who has turned and made the mighty hunter to stand, facing the winged one, who made the blackness coming on wings and turned day into night, who calls upon the water so make the sea to pour out over the face of the earth, and the earthquake like a leaf in the wind. It is I, the Lord, who lays low all other gods before me who will do this. I will cause the wife to come to light, and the husband to be made righteous." There was a notation that a piece was missing before continuing. "'I will make the way straight, and I will reveal my right arm of righteousness, holy to save, for I above all nations will reign in righteousness, and my people will be a royal priesthood teaching all countries of my salvation. I shall make a way in the desert,' said the Lord, 'I will make straight in the wilderness a highway. Therefore, my people repent, lay prostrate before me, trusting in my mercy and goodness.'"

A thought crossed Travis's mind that made his eyes light up. Travis dropped the paper he was holding and said, "The constellation that has Orion as its belt is the hunter, and from what this is saying, it calls him Michael. But what does confuse me is that Orion has always been laying on its side in the southern part of the constellations," he said, picking up the paper off the floor and handing it back to John.

John grabbed Gideon's Bible from the nightstand by the bed and thumbed through it. He came to the place which he was looking for. Quoting, "Daniel 12:1 At that time, Michael shall stand up, the great prince which standeth for the children of thy people; and there shall be a time of trouble, such as never was since there was a nation even to that same time: and at that time thy people shall be delivered, everyone who is found written in the book." And with that, he put the Bible down. "I thought I read it somewhere."

James, who had been listening while he was working, turned to the boys and said, "I think we need to take a break here and have something to eat. How about you clear off a spot on the bed since I have taken up the table. That ways I do not have to move the scroll unduly," he said the boys cleared off a spot. Soon everyone was eating in silence, thinking about what they had just uncovered. There wasn't much talk except for a "pass this or that" and "thank you."

It was later the next day when the earth started quaking, pipes started creaking, wires started singing and crackling, and the day started getting dark. It was a mad scramble for all of them to gather up their stuff and run out of the building before it collapsed. Looking up, they saw the start of what looked to be an eclipse, except you could see fiery wings on each side. Travis pointed excitedly at it, saying, "It is Niribu; take off all magnetic material and lay down flat over there in the clearing. What we are about to witness is the end of our world, for we are in the path of a total eclipse by Niribu as it heads our way. Given its current position, we might as well kiss our asses goodbye. That great big fiery ball with wings that you see in the sky has a magnetic pull which will only increase as it gets closer. When it hits, it will blow Earth to smithereens," he said, trying to be heard above the howling winds. Objects were being lifted off and carried away by the magnetic pull and the whirlwinds that grew in intensity as the Earth's shaking grew in power. People were hanging on to anything, the building was collapsing, and all magnetic parts were flying off everywhere. The earth continued to shake in ever-increasing viciousness reducing everything to dust and rubble. People were being carried away by the whirlwinds, screaming in the wind, and still, the darkness grew as Niribu drew closer. On howled the winds as the four hung on to the rock, they found themselves on. Pipes came out of the earth and flew off, fires exploded, and water gushed at the sites of what remained. Vehicles lifted off the ground and were taken up and out of sight, the hair stood on end, the air sizzled and cracked, and still, they could cling to the rock they laid on.

The land started to wave and heave like water lapping on a beach, leveling buildings and the land itself. Lightning cracked across the sky, lighting up the earth every time it streaked. With loud rumblings and the roar of a dozen waterfalls, the sky rolled back and forth with clouds clashing violently together. It was when the sky lit up from another burst of lightning, brighter than even on the most auspicious day, lit up the earth in an unearthly blue-white light, that all they were able to see through the flying debris the earth flattened out and moved in waves, quaking as if shivering in the cold. Then just as fast as it was light, it was darker than the darkest deep cave where no light was seen except the dark red angry Niribu flying in fast on its fiery wings, getting larger and larger by the moment.

All of them were now praying in their own way. With the words of the Lord so recently translated running through their heads. They repented, lying prostrate and hoping God indeed was in control and was mighty enough to save. Laying close to the ground, there seemed to be a gap between earth and winds where gravity could still hold them down to land. There they lay, waiting for the world to end and praying that it wouldn't.

It was at the next lightning streaking across the sky that Travis looked over towards the southern horizon, grabbed John's arm, and pulled to get his attention. But before he could do anything more, it was dark once again. In the darkness, he tried to be heard over the howling banshee of the winds. By slowly creeping together until they were just heads in the center of a circle, were they able to find quietness during the storm so that they could hear Travis? At the next lightning, he pointed to the south, screaming his words hoping they would not be carried away by the wind. "Look at the hunter constellation; our Earth has so tilted that it makes him look like he is standing up."

It was not until the next lightning that John could see what Travis was pointing out, and he could only catch a few words. Flashing lightning flashing across the sky was like a strobe light at a disco dance was able to get his father to look in the same direction from under his arm and down past his toes. Professor James did not catch on at first what the boys were pointing to until he heard John scream, "Orion," and he saw it was the prophecy coming true. Michael, the hunter, was standing in the Southern Hemisphere, his feet touching the ground. Watching the spot, they saw the earth crack open the mountain. They all saw it; Michael's right foot was on the mountain. Travis peeked up to see where Niribu was and was surprised to know that it was no longer where it was just moments ago. In fact, watching Niribu for a while, he noticed it was not any more prominent. In fact, it seemed to be suspended from advancing any closer.

John called out, "Look, look at the mountain!" Bright bluish light was shooting straight up from the mountain into the sky. It had a column like a vast lit-up tornado, and before it was debris sweeping to the left and the right as if an invisible broom was clearing a path before it. The winds died. Everything seemed suspended, no earth quaking, no winds, and even Niribu seemed frozen to its spot in the sky. Those people who had survived were starting to rise up, and all turned to the coming column of bluish-white light. As it entered Jerusalem, everyone could see the Ark of the Covenant arriving as if gliding on air; the mercy seat cover was off and following as if being carried by invisible hands. People could see the sapphire tablets of stone refracting the bluish light straight up. As it passed where they stood, James could decipher the writing, just as it had been recorded in the Bible.

Everyone was filled with awe and wonderment. People fell on their knees as it passed, keeping a safe distance to not touch it, and followed in its path after it passed. It continued until it had arrived just north of where the Dome of the Rock once was. There it came to rest as if gently set down. The lid came to rest beside it. The Sapphire tablets rested on top of the Ark of the Covenant. The bluish-lit column continued to shine way out into the sky. And when they looked back up, they saw another planet from the east, across the face of Niribu, towards the column of bluish light and continue west, slinging Niribu into a new direction away from Earth. Niribu took out any near objects in its path as it went. X366 fragmented upon impact. Fireworks lit the sky as the fragments fell towards earth.

Brings the sun into clear view as Niribu headed out. They now saw that the sun was larger than life, moving somewhat faster and out of position, taking a new path across the sky. This world was no longer recognizable, with everything out of place, and all bearings seemed gone. The sun was way brighter than before, and it hurt the eyes so much that everyone kept their eyes shielded and looked down.

People were scurrying for what cover they could find as the sun continued to beat down upon them from its new position. Travis, John, and James immediately dug into soil with their bare hands, a trench deep enough to create shade and protect them from the sun. Once all had crawled in and settled down, Travis peeked over the mound and, using his fingers against the horizon, estimated the new distance and positions. He was doing guesstimates using triangulations of whatever bearing he could ascertain. Soon John and the Professor were drawn in, trying to help him with approximations of the distance of one object to another. Within hours it was evening, and the sun was now setting in what once was north.

Finally, Travis leaned back and said, "Ok, based on the fact that we all agree that in the general area of the north, the sun is heading for a sunset, based on the agreement that we all believe the sun is traveling faster, and the obvious fact, that it is closer to Earth. I would say that we now have a new north and South Pole. And if my suspicions are correct, we will see the sunrise from the direction of Egypt tomorrow morning."

John had been thinking about what had occurred and said, "That is not all we have," pointing to the Ark of the Covenant, which was no longer refracting the bluish light, where people of all faiths were gathering to worship and pray. "The religious paradigm that we use to know has just been blown out of its water. What really scares me is how true the scroll was."

James took a deep breath and sighed, "I know I am a changed man. I know that whatever is going to happen now, this will change some forever, while others will only think of this as a hiccup in their plans. It is those others that I worry about."

Picking themselves up out of the dirt, they headed into the sunset with John pointing again back at the Ark of the Covenant, saying, "I know where the Jews will be building their temple." And with that, they all chuckled.

THE END

www.ingramcontent.com/pod-product-compliance
Lightning Source LLC
LaVergne TN
LVHW041935070526
838199LV00051BA/2800